D0200817

WITHDRAWN

WILD JUSTICE

Books by Loren D. Estleman

*Published by Tom Doherty Associates

WILD
JUSTICE

Loren D. Estleman

A TOM DOHERTY ASSOCIATES BOOK
NEW YORK

WILD JUSTICE

Copyright © 2018 by Loren D. Estleman

A Forge Book
Published by Tom Doherty Associates
175 Fifth Avenue
New York, NY 10010

www.tor-forge.com

Forge® is a registered trademark of Macmillan Publishing Group, LLC.

The Library of Congress Cataloging-in-Publication Data
is available upon request.

ISBN 978-1-250-19709-2 (hardcover)
ISBN 978-1-250-19719-1 (ebook)

Our books may be purchased in bulk for promotional, educational, or business
use. Please contact your local bookseller or the Macmillan Corporate and
Premium Sales Department at 1-800-221-7945, extension 5442, or by email at
MacmillanSpecialMarkets@macmillan.com.

First Edition: November 2018

Printed in the United States of America

0 9 8 7 6 5 4 3 2 1

PHIL ROSETTE
(1948–2017)

Soldier, writer, husband, father, friend;
in any order you wish

Revenge is a kind of wild justice, which the more man's nature runs to, the more ought law to weed it out.

—Francis Bacon

WILD
JUSTICE

I

THE JUDGE HEADS EAST

ONE

—

He **died pronouncing** sentence in a double-homicide. The defense kept the appeals process going for six months because no one could agree on which hit the bench first, his gavel or his head.

That spring of 1896, Harlan A. Blackthorne had been the law in Montana for thirty years, its first federal judge and the last to claim complete jurisdiction over a territory the size of Spain. His presidential appointment limited his authority to crimes committed against the United States: mail-train robberies, Indian depredations, murders of federal employees crowning the list. Within days of donning the robes, he'd expanded that responsibility to include domestic killings, claim-jumping, goldbricking, road-agentry, and rape. Few complained: certainly not the overworked circuit judges whose swollen dockets he'd plundered, or the peace officers who were paid by the mile to deliver their captives to the territorial capital in Helena, or the victims and survivors of victims who kept track of the long-term and death sentences the carpet-bagger from Washington handed out the way a Christian charity distributed King James Bibles.

His rivals in Congress launched periodic campaigns— usually at election time—to unseat him for overstepping his boundaries and downright abuse of power (of both of which he was guilty), but he'd served two terms there himself, collecting markers from some colleagues. A well-placed wire plowed a path through carloads of taxpayer-financed letters to constituents, filled as they were with righteous wrath on their account, like a locomotive through bone china. In this way (and with a dollop of old-fashioned Yankee blackmail), the Judge sat secure in his seat under seven presidents.

The harassment didn't stop with politics. Broadsides sprang up throughout the frontier offering as much as ten thousand dollars for Blackthorne's head, pledged by an uneasy coalition of robber barons, big-time rustlers, bushwhackers, redlegs, copperheads, rumrunners, gunrunners, and a well-known Chicago meatpacker driven into receivership by the Judge's enforcement of the quarantine on Texas cattle. The brains behind the bounty belonged to a ninety-pound pimp nick-named Little Great Falls, who'd conducted personal business dealings with all the parties involved; they anted up the reward from their own treasuries. Although it was posted anonymously, all their names were known to their quarry within weeks. The men Blackthorne had recruited to enforce his decisions maintained an effective network of river-rats and spies scattered throughout the outlaw world.

He did nothing about it personally. He didn't have to.

His first act after settling in was to rag Washington for the funds necessary to assemble a platoon of deputies to assist the

U.S. marshal appointed by President Andrew Johnson in maintaining the peace. Conceived in idealism but carried out pragmatically, this company consisted largely of men indistinguishable from those they were charged to bring to bear; with some lawmen of legitimate experience leavened in to establish order and placate the press.

They were not men to let the grass grow.

Having read accounts in the daily journals of his fellow financiers shot to death while resisting arrest, and of the unexpected suicide of the personal representative of a Chicago magnate in his hotel room in Deer Lodge, Little Great Falls decamped in haste to old Mexico, where he was cut to pieces by a woman he'd gone into business with in a Sonoran bawdyhouse.

When the character of many of his centurions came to light, and the opposition press cried for an investigation, Blackthorne was sanguine: "It isn't sufficient merely to comb out the lice; the treatment to eradicate them is necessarily caustic." In time, when it was noted that the names of marauders that had become fixtures in the newspapers had fallen away through conviction, execution, and an excess of lead in their diet, the cries ceased.

Blackthorne was small but rangy, with a big head made larger still by a rich growth of black hair and a Vandyke beard, never allowed to gray. His suits were tailored and cut for a younger man—and a dandy at that—but he took care of them so that they made fewer demands on his salary than a mail-order rig built to withstand ten years of daily wear. Several attempts to expose him as an embezzler based on his finery dashed themselves to pieces against the solid rock of his meticulous bookkeeping; cavalier as he was about his exercise of power, when it came to money he was as scrupulous as a spinster aunt. He'd supported himself during his unpaid apprenticeship with a Philadelphia law firm working for blacksmiths and wheelwrights, and in the last year of his life, when he'd drunk enough of his good imported Highland Scotch whiskey, could still out-arm-wrestle a fit man half his age when challenged beyond ignoring.

He'd passed the bar on a course of his own study and still owned the thumb-soiled volumes of Blackstone he'd bought one by one with what he'd managed to save living in a cold-water flat and bringing his luncheon to work; no two of them belonged to the same matched set. They'd made the journey with him to Washington and eventually Montana Territory in his army rucksack. His only vanity apart from how he dressed himself was the set of ivory teeth he'd had made to take the place of the ones he'd lost to the fighting and the fare south of the border. (He insisted they'd been carved by hand from the keys of a piano abandoned along the Oregon Trail; but I'd seen the box he kept them in when he wasn't wearing them, and it bore the name of a pharmaceutical manufactory in Boston stamped in gold.) He was devoted to his wife, a plump beauty when they'd met, but who'd grown absolutely stout by the time I knew her. He himself maintained his own lean figure by walking the heels off any subordinate who was fool enough to join him on his daily constitutional.

The lawless population hated him with the passion of a religious zealot. The Montanans old enough to remember what the place was like before he came, a wild, wooded, virtually unsettled wilderness, full of deep gorges and dense growth made to order for vermin to seek cover in, worshipped him in like measure. Easterners thrilled to read of his marshals' bloody skirmishes and the swift thistled shock of his hangmen's ropes snapping the spines of the unredeemed in the wire columns of *The New York Sun*, *The Chicago Tribune*, *The Boston Journal*, and in *Harper's Weekly*, secure in the thousands of miles that separated them from the events. His rivals schemed around the clock trying to find a way to tear him from his roots, or at least keep him too busy defending himself to pursue his offenses against the organized system of justice, but that same vast distance took the edge off every swing they took; by the time they gathered themselves to react to his most recent outrage, it was weeks old. As well pot at a star hundreds of years after its latest twinkle.

What did I think of him? I, who'd worked with him hand-in-glove longer than all the rest, and who knew him better than anyone—including Mrs. Blackthorne? He was a first-class son of a bitch. But how many men have you known who were first in their class at anything?

TWO

I got the word while waiting my turn in the chair at the King Alexander, the Judge's own tonsorial parlor. I was fresh back from Idaho and one of his wild-goose chases. The years had taken their toll; every muscle I had was threatening to secede and after three soakings in the Cathay Gardens I still smelled like an old cracked boot. I was determined to draw my bonus by charging the works, lavender and all, to Blackthorne's account. *The Independent* was trying to work up an uprising in the Lapwai Indian Reservation for the purpose of boosting circulation, so the discussion between the barber and the man he was shearing came filtered through my reading.

"'Hanged by the neck until you are dead.' His last words, so they say. Not too much round the ears, Minos. You made me look like a Mormon last time."

Two other customers were ahead of me, one immersed in *The Police Gazette*, the other fiddling with a cigar. They, the

man in the chair, and the barber, a burly Greek whose bald
head resembled an egg resting in a nest of salt-and-pepper facial
growth, looked my way when I crackled the newspaper.

"*Whose* last words?" I said; although there was only one
man for five hundred miles who could claim clear title to the
phrase. I'd heard it a couple of dozen times when duty forced
me to attend proceedings in capital cases.

The man, a telegraph clerk I recognized but whose name I'd
never heard, agreed. "Well, who else? Old Scratch will have to
fight for his seat now."

Not everyone in town shared a good opinion of the Judge.
He was impatient with incompetence and sloth and took no
pains to conceal the fact, and I knew from experience the clerk
couldn't spell *cat* with Noah Webster at his side.

"The hell you say."

"You calling me a liar?"

"I don't know you well enough to say either way. Who did it?"

That went over well with the audience. When the belly
laughs receded, the clerk in the chair blew his nose on the sheet
covering him. "Well, you can pin that one on the Almighty, if
you can get Him into the dock. But who's to sit in judgment
on Him with the old goat dead?"

I left the shop then. Even if Blackthorne's credit hadn't run
out with his passing, there would be no entertainment in sticking his estate with the bill. I went from there to Chicago Joe's,
drank a hole through the middle of the afternoon, and may
have spent some time upstairs with one or two of the hired
girls; but the day was such a swirl of aching joints, sour-mash
fumes, shrill laughter (some of it maybe mine), and the hurdy-
gurdy of a tin-tack piano with one dead key, I can't swear to
anything; although I have a vague picture of the back of my
hand stroking a raw patch where I'd scraped a powdered cheek

with my stubble, and of adding a cartwheel dollar to the others on a chest of drawers by way of apology.

Was I sad, relieved, or just struck stupid? The last, definitely. Had the Judge outfoxed the Mexican Army, both houses of Congress, and the entire outlaw population of Montana only to fall victim to divine will, like any common mortal? It was like looking west and finding the Rockies gone, leaving open plain all the way to the Pacific.

But I was back in my room, relatively sober, when the messenger came from the Widow Blackthorne.

"*Delaware?*" **I had** to get it out of my mouth. It tasted strange.

Beatrice Blackthorne jerked a nod. Her wattles kept moving for a season after. "Delaware, yes. He was born there. His family plot is there, and it's where he intended to be buried; and I alongside, when it comes my time. Thirty years in this savage place are penance sufficient. Whatever his sins, eternity seems excessive, or don't you agree?"

It was my turn to nod, and let her take that as a sign of concurrence; although if she cared to untangle her own language it could just as easily go the other direction.

It didn't surprise me that she had no ambition to lay her husband to rest in Helena. She'd never made a secret of her contempt for the town or its citizens or the territory—now the state—where it was located. What took me back was the place of his birth. That the Judge was a Yankee was the commonly accepted wisdom in a community divided between diehard Southern sympathizers and Union loyalists; that he should have come from the first state to ratify the U.S. Constitution—and therefore the most Yankee of all the Yankee states—

seemed like rubbing the nose of the Confederacy in the thoroughness of its defeat.

Although he was far from the most diplomatic of men, he'd parried all questions concerning his true origins all these years; there were even some who suspected he'd hailed from one of those border regions where to declare an opinion for or against States' Rights, or to hesitate over the subject, was to invite personal injury. I'd heard he was the son of an un-lettered Missouri farmer; but people will spin a tale just to plug a gap.

To me it didn't signify. I'd fought for the Union and had put the war ten years behind when I came to serve the court, in-tending to drift on after eight or ten months, twenty-one years ago. I had to admire this fresh reminder of the almighty strength of his resolve. Apart from the odd itinerant repertory troupe or medicine show, the sole diversion in early days was to wheedle out the life story of every stranger who wandered into town. A holdout of ten minutes was regarded the record. Three decades of silence belonged to the fantastic romances of Mr. Jules Verne.

I assumed she was confiding in me this guilty secret just to pass the hour before it was time to leave for the Benedictine Brothers Mortuary to sit in vigil with the remains and greet visitors who came to pay their respects. (The contract to pre-pare and usually bury condemned parties and prisoners who'd died in custody belonged to Hieronymus Japes & Sons, Undertakers, at government expense; but the Widow Black-thorne would have none of that.) We were by no means on intimate terms. She kept her distance from everyone connected with the court, excepting Erasmus Callaway, the U.S. prose-cutor, and his wife, Dorcas, with whom the Blackthornes had attended church services. I'd been surprised she'd ask me to escort her and accompany her throughout the ordeal, and that she'd even known my name.

We sat in the close twilit parlor of the house she'd shared with her husband on a hill overlooking most of the city, chock-ablock with hard shield-back chairs, pedestal tables, lamps, layers of figured rugs, a pianoforte with chaste pantaloons cloaking its legs, and the smell of moth flakes. Most of the furniture had come, like the owners themselves, partway by rail, then aboard steamboats, ferries, coaches, and freight wagons in the days before the Northern Pacific track gangs discovered the vast black rectangle that stood between Wyoming Territory and the Dominion of Canada. I doubted the Judge had spent much time in that room. His tastes ran toward deep horsehair armchairs, plain oak, good cigars, peaty spirits, and auld Scottish hymns played on the great pipe organ in St. Sebastian's Presbyterian Church.

"Harlan and I embark for Wilmington morning after tomorrow," she said, breaking a long silence punctuated by the dry tick-t-t-tock of a Regulator clock; its speech impediment stood my skin-cells on edge. "You will be at the station at eight-fifteen."

That cracked me loose from my stupor. "Nothing would please me more, ma'am, but the porters are more than capable of loading your luggage." Which would include the Judge himself, in a rough cedar box. A peacock in life, the old hypocrite had left instructions to be committed to the earth in the humblest of shells; as if the show of meekness would take in his Maker.

"I am sure they are. You will accompany me on the journey home."

I'd spent that stuffy conversational lull stewing over where I'd go and what work I'd take up now; the midget magistrates Grover Cleveland would likely appoint to fill the void offered no incentive to stay on, and if the truth be told I was tired of haring after felons. Blackthorne, half-teasing, had threatened more than once to put me up for U.S. marshal, but desk duty was worse than riding fence, which itself was no match for a bullet in the brain, inflicted by myself. On the other hand, the cattle business was a young man's work, and the choices there were narrowing by the day as eastern conglomerates moved in on what was left of the open range, making do with fewer hands at lower pay. I was too old to have a dog in that fight.

All that considered, Delaware had reckoned nowhere in the muddle. I was born in a trapper's shack high in the Bitterroots. Cold Harbor, Virginia, was as far as I'd ever wandered from there, and I'd been too busy dodging Confederate grapeshot to study the culture. I'd never learn the language.

"Thank you for your faith, Mrs. Blackthorne. Any of the other deputies would serve as well or better. Jack Truewell was employed by the Pinkertons as a bodyguard. He got Jay Gould through the Panic alive, and he reads poetry."

"I was not aware of Mr. Truewell or his virtues. However, he is not the man my husband requested."

"Requested?"

"In his letter of intent, witnessed by Mr. Gottlieb, his bailiff, and placed in Mr. Callaway's safe, to be consulted in the event of his decease. Along with this." She drew an envelope from the drawer of the drum table at her elbow and held it out.

I took it, goose that I was. It was small, about four by three inches, made of the heavy rag bond he'd ordered to replace the stationery used by his predecessors, j.p.'s who requisitioned coarse wood-fiber paper from the local mill, charged the absentee territorial governor for good vellum, and pocketed the difference. *Page Murdock* was written on it in the Judge's jagged, slashing hand. I broke the plain wax seal with a thumb and unfolded the contents with the name of the federal court embossed on the letterhead. More of that same impatient script followed.

"Dear Page," it began, and my heart sank. He'd addressed me by my Christian name only when he had some particularly unpleasant duty in mind. It had invariably come with my life in more danger than usual.

> Since you're reading this [he wrote], I'm dead, and you, in defiance of all the odds have survived me. Congratulations.
>
> Beatrice—who doubtless will bury us all—will have broken the glad news that you are to join us on the pilgrimage to the place of my eternal rest.
>
> I employ the phrase "glad news" without irony. Throughout the long term of our professional relationship, fate has demonstrated that every assignment you have undertaken on behalf of myself and the people whom I serve has provided a welcome distraction from your monotonous existence as a friend of the court. I have no reason to believe that this latest will disappoint.
>
> I leave you, the boldest of all my knights, with this one last adventure. Savor it, as it's unlikely any others will come along to compare.
>
> > Yours most sincerely,
> > The Honorable Harlan Amsdill Blackthorne

Knights; he put it in writing, and on the threshold before coming face-to-face with the Great Imponderable, in one fell swoop paying me one of his damned satirical compliments and crowning himself King Arthur.

What did I tell you? A first-class son of a bitch.

THREE

The visitation at Benedictine's was private, reserved for friends and close associates. The following morning the Judge was removed to the courthouse—whose bricks he'd practically laid single-handed—where he reposed in state throughout the day while hundreds of mourners passed, pausing briefly to look at the small man in the plain box, then were chivvied along to make room for the others, the way they said the Beefeaters prodded tourists past the Crown Jewels in the Tower of London.

Some came to gaze one last time upon the features that had for so long represented the face of justice in Montana, others to see them for the first time. Men in frock coats and faded flannel, ruffles and overalls, hand-lasted boots and Montgomery Ward's brogans peeling at the toes, women carrying babies, whole families. (Ma and Pa grabbing Junior by the arm and thrusting him up to the bier: "Remember, boy! The Great Man himself! There'll never be another like him. Hanged little boys who didn't clean their plates and wouldn't go to bed when they were told. See that broad brow, the whiskers of a philosopher. Commit every last detail to memory so's you can tell your grandchildren what they missed. Now run on home and shovel out the barn.") The line stretched out the door, down the street, and around the corner for a quarter-mile. The crowd was kept inside the bounds of good manners by a detachment of mounted city policemen, pound-for-pound the worst horsemen west of anywhere, but their horses were too fat and lazy to take advantage of it.

Not everyone had come to pay homage; which was where E. Z. Gottlieb, Blackthorne's bailiff, earned his day's dollar. He stood five feet, five inches in his thick-soled boots, a solid fire-plug of a man in starched gray twill and glistening Sam Browne belt, a proper harness bull, gripping a hickory truncheon in both fists across his waist, eyes restlessly prowling the line all the way to the street. The moment he spotted a face from his mental identity file of known "wrong-os," or a stranger who fidgeted and kept looking around to see who was watching, Gottlieb would leave his station, approach the party, and shielding the motion from the others with his square body, ram the truncheon so deep in the man's belly the fellow had no choice but to flee outside to avoid disgracing himself by vomiting in public. Whether he'd come just to spit on the guest of honor, or to work more sinister mischief, was all the same to the bailiff; he'd brook no breach of the ceremony's dignity. In the six years the little troll had served the court, putting down commotions of every description, I'd never seen him draw his sidearm, or actually swing his club; in his hands it was a lance, not a bludgeon, the act performed underhand, with minimum effort to maximum effect. He could kill a man

that way if he chose—or if he just miscalculated. The latter
event was the more unlikely.

All the deputy marshals—those not out on assignment—
showed up to file past in their turn. They wore the homely
cut-out star in a pin-on shield with its dull finish, with a thin
black ribbon tied around it in a simple bow. An entrepreneur-
ial local tailor had placed a black-bordered notice in *The Herald*,
offering the bow, pre-tied, to sworn officers at the special dis-
count price of a penny apiece. It didn't cover the cost of the
advertisement, but it provided an opportunity to acquaint the
customer with the other goods he had in stock. Once the first
of them appeared wearing this sign of respect, of course the
rest had to follow suit, myself included; although I wasn't as
uncomfortable with the bit of fluff as I was with the badge itself. I hadn't worn it since the day I was sworn in. It caught the
light and made a mark to shoot at.

Some attended who had retired from the marshals' service.
I recognized a few of the old guard—a number of them
younger than I—from personal acquaintance, identified others
by their posture, their gait (a kind of sailor's roll, developed in
the saddle), the way their gaze swept the room directly upon
entrance, the flat weary tragedy in their eyes, like weathered
tombstones erected over the remains of their ideals. I saw it
every day I shaved, when I had the luxury of a looking-glass.
Men old before their time; not beasts, but no longer quite
human, and a long way from certain that survival was worth
its price. They didn't wear the ribbon. They had no star to wind
it around, having turned it in when they resigned. I wondered
whether they'd have worn it in any case.

The ribbon was profiteering, plain and simple; but it was
discreet compared to the trinkets and *cartes de visite* that were
being hammered out, put up in windows, and hawked on the

street to capitalize on the solemn proceedings. Some of the visitors fanned themselves with palm-shaped paper cutouts promoting the Benedictine Brothers Mortuary in respectable black capitals without serifs. Bruno, youngest of the clan, stood outside the door to hand them out. The day was unseasonably warm for April and the air hung heavy inside.

So the day wore on, soporifically and in near-silence, the shuffling feet and low murmurs swallowed by the coffered ceiling, fractured at every hour and half hour by the tolling of the three-thousand-pound bell in the clock tower.

"Barbaric."

I looked at Mrs. Blackthorne beside me, seated in a wicker chair to spare her the ordeal of standing to accept condolences from those who chose to approach. She'd barely breathed the word, and I couldn't tell if she even knew she'd said it aloud. Nor could I decide if she was passing judgment on the fans and other frippery or on the entire affair. In her weeds, a heavy veil concealing her face, she made a black blot like the ones the Judge had made when he overloaded his pen before signing a death certificate or an eviction order.

On her other side, hands folded at his waist, stood Eugene Staples, the current federal marshal. He'd been in office only six months, and I hadn't enough experience of him yet to take his measure. He was young, had had something to do with getting out the Democratic vote in Cincinnati or somesuch place in the last election, although not enough for a plum plundering appointment like collector of the tariff, but if he resented being exiled to the back of beyond he was stoic enough not to show it. His expression seemed passive, as if he too was pondering his future now; as I said, I hadn't the chance to study him to confirm anything based on appearances. Maybe he was wondering if the Chinese laundrywoman the Judge recommended to all his people would scorch his shirts. (She would; I took mine to an Armenian across from the library.)

I performed my wooden-Indian act without rancor, only boredom; which contrary to what you may have read in *Beadle's Dime Library* comprised most of the work in keeping the peace. I'd already had my look at the exhibit, yesterday at the mortuary and again when I'd arrived at the courthouse riding with Mrs. Blackthorne in her phaeton. He lay with a velvet cushion supporting his head, an old eagle in profile with his hair and beard combed the way he'd worn them in life— the widow had directed that part of the operation personally— in his favorite mulberry-colored Prince Albert coat and gray figured waistcoat with a platinum watch chain describing a *W* across his spare belly, hands folded on Maine's *Ancient Law*, a slim volume bound in worn supple leather. A pin of native quartz fixed his cravat to his shirt (*The Independent*, an opposition newspaper, would call it a "two-carat diamond," with all that implied). His fob was the stylized square-and-calipers of the Freemasons and his belt fastened with the buckle he'd had made from the medal of valor he'd earned in Mexico; or so he'd claimed.

At first glance the day before, it had looked like the Judge, then it hadn't. It had taken me most of an hour to nail down what was wrong. He'd worn the tight-lipped smile I knew too well, but the Benedictine who'd shaped it had neglected to take out his teeth. He'd worn them only when court was in session, where he'd maintained the stony mien of a vengeful pagan god carved from granite. They must have been as uncomfortable to manage as a mouthful of marbles; whether they'd contributed to the severity of his decisions might have exposed the trials to review, although none of his officers, knowing the

cases as well as they did, let a word of the situation reach anyone outside the service.

This morning, I saw that his wife (it could have been no one
else) had corrected that. Now he looked eerily natural, as if he
might open his eyes any time and skewer me with that dia-
bolical grimace that masqueraded as amusement. I almost
wished the adjustment hadn't been made. With the ivories
pushing out the lower half of his face he'd appeared almost
comical, as if he'd forgotten to swallow the canary.

Which I'd taken as a lucky sign. If the old ogre came back
to haunt anyone, it would be the undertaker.

But even after all those years I still hadn't plumbed him to
his depth. I was, and am still, the primary target of his ghost.

FOUR

The locomotive was a monster, big as a bunkhouse, ten feet tall at the cab by twenty-five long from coupling to cowcatcher, black and hot and glistening with oil, inhaling and exhaling steam in a husky cadenced rhythm like a buffalo bull sleeping on its side. Ten or so years earlier I'd lived aboard a train for weeks, slicing through the heart of the most primitive region of old Mexico on a mission of assassination sanctioned by Blackthorne; but that engine, tough little nut that it was, had borne no more resemblance to this one than a baby carriage did to a beer wagon.

The rig seemed excessive considering what it was pulling: the tender, a day coach, a dining car, a Pullman sleeper, and the caboose, which was where the Judge would be riding, his veins pumped full of embalming agent, practically a wax replica of the original. Red-white-and-blue bunting swagged the sides of the passenger cars just below the windows, with black crepe twisted cunningly around it, in case some uneducated observers might mistake it for a whistle-stop campaign vehicle for some presidential hopeful. It still struck me as gay for the journey's purpose. I couldn't see Beatrice Blackthorne's hand in it. Callaway, the federal prosecutor, had made all the arrangements, including wiring ahead to every major city we'd be passing through, partly out of respect and partly as a pre-launch maneuver in his race for governor. The Judge's funeral train was his version of a black ribbon.

It would get worse.

I couldn't foresee it then, and maybe Callaway couldn't either. Blackthorne's command over his pet bull terrier would grow fainter with each mile that separated the one from the cadaver of the other, and the lawyer's boldness increase from tie to tie.

We—that is, the widow—did manage to best him on one point. When Callaway suggested that a party of married deputy marshals and their wives join us aboard, in the interest of avoiding unseemly suggestions concerning the spectacle of a bereaved matron traveling with a single officer unchaperoned, the bereaved matron cut him off, as abruptly as her late husband quelled disturbances in his courtroom.

"I am seventy, Erasmus. I put away such things long before you came here. Did you think thirty years of name-calling, finger-pointing, calumny, and offensive caricatures in the press were borne by Harlan alone? The infernal responsibilities of his office drove him early to his grave. [I held my tongue at this point in her harangue; she and Holy Scripture differed on the subject of man's allotted span.] If the jackals are still unsatisfied and would turn their slings and arrows upon his widow, does it not reflect more upon their characters than mine? And who are we to prevent an ass from exposing himself as an ass?"

I'd heard the old man say something along the same lines more than once: "Never interrupt an enemy while he's making a fatal mistake." Callaway went pale to the roots of his burnsides and said no more on the matter. They were more words than I'd heard her express in twenty-one years. For the first time I realized the extent of the part she'd played in forging the iron fist that had pounded the law so deep into an untamed territory.

The train was an express, the way cleared along the entire route by order of the cabinet official in charge, stopping only to take on wood and water and give the yokels along the way the chance to crane their necks at the vessel transporting the Judge's mortal coil. No one was to board except reporters connected with journals selected by a lottery draw, and they were permitted only to observe, photograph, and sketch the plank box; Mrs. Blackthorne was not to be bothered unless she invited an interview.

The third member of our party, not counting a superfluous conductor, was our cook. In this, my companion had acquiesced to the prosecutor's wishes. She'd intended to use the services of Henry, a convicted bigamist and a Negro the Judge had released from the territorial prison and employed as the couple's personal chef. But his face, disfigured by a scar from surgery to remove a tumor from his cheek, lifting a corner of his lip into a snarl, might cast a sinister shadow on the enterprise if a photographer should happen to capture it through a window. The job fell to Caspar, from the kitchen of the Last Chance Hotel. He was afflicted as well, although not in a way that was visible so long as he kept his mouth closed. As the story went, after failing the seminary back East, he'd drifted in a whiskey fog into a house of doubtful reputation in St. Louis, where to spare himself from the sin of lust he bit off his tongue.

"Caspar's the superior baker, so I saw no cause to object," Beatrice confided to me. "There is an advantage to be gained by letting Erasmus think he has won."

I responded with a shrug. Serpentine thinking was the Blackthornes' strong suit, not mine. At all events it hardly mattered that the hotel chef couldn't speak, as I doubted we had much to talk about.

The funeral service, in the evening following the display in the courthouse, had dragged on, with one luminary and near-luminary after the other grappling his way to the altar in St. Sebastian's to stake his claim to a special acquaintance with the departed, some lively passages from Revelation—the Judge's preferred book of the New Testament, gloomy as it was, and certainly approved by the fighting pastor, and enough "braes" and "bairns" sung by a paroled tenor to the accompaniment of the booming organ to run Robbie Burns himself out into the street to rest his ears. No bagpipes, praise God; that was one opinion the old man and I shared.

The congregation, which had been lulled into a stupor by lyrics belonging to a language that meant as much to most of those assembled as back-country Farsi, perked up when the opening chords sounded of a song that had swept the continent from coast to coast for five years, and then that clear piping ex-convict voice sang:

> After the ball is over;
> after the break of morn,
> After the dancers' leaving,
> After the stars are gone.

Many a heart is aching,
if you could read them all;
Many the hopes that have vanished,
After the ball.

The tune had taken the Judge's fancy—which rarely directed itself toward anything that smacked even slightly of novelty—the first time he'd encountered it. He'd been overheard humming the melody between witness testimonies and while studying transcripts in his chambers, and on the occasion of their fortieth anniversary his wife had presented him with a perforated disk that played it on the music box in their parlor soon after it became available. The song, about good things ending but their sweetness lingering on like a regretful ghost, contained just the sort of romantic melancholy that appealed to a man of his character.

Had I known how many more times I'd be forced to listen to that blasted air over the next two weeks, I'd have hunted down every publisher that issued it on music sheets and burned the building to the ground.

The first chorus was the signal for the pallbearers to take their stations. We were all six deputy marshals, and we all knew one another, with varying degrees of liking and respect—starting at zero—but every one long in the service, the longest being myself. We stood in our frock coats and white cotton gloves while the pastor slid the cushion from behind Blackthorne's head, laid him flat, and placed the lid on the box, separating us from him for the last time. I felt a tug—of fresh resentment. I'd drawn front right; those damn instructions again, as if I hadn't carried the old devil on my shoulder for most of a generation. I was surprised, however, when we took hold of the strap handles and hoisted the box, at how little it weighed. He'd held down the lid on the boiling kettle of the last circle of hell for so long it should have been like carrying a thousandweight of pig iron. I was convinced then, if any such confirmation was needed, of the existence of the soul, and that it had substance, noticeably missing from its parcel on earth.

He left the church, as he had every Sunday for three decades, but this time to the strains of a ballad still popular in New York City, Chicago, St. Louis, and San Francisco, and not under his own steam. Laverne Waters' hearse, a fine one of black lacquer and glass panes, with drawn sere curtains, rubber tires, and the only team of matched whites this side of Pierre, was waiting out front. In early days, when the turnover in the population was less frequent, Waters had made the vehicle serve double-duty as a jitney taking passengers to and from the train station, but the city had grown to the point where he made a steady living renting it out to all the local morticians. That had deprived the citizens of the entertainment of observing newcomers' reactions upon finding a funeral wagon ready to convey them to their lodgings; but such is progress.

We half-dozen followed it at a walking pace to the station, trailing the mourners behind us, some on foot, some in vehicles, with the widow and the pastor leading in her phaeton, and the Lewis and Clark County Marching Band playing refrain after refrain of "After the Ball" at the rear. The boardwalks, doorways, and balconies on both sides of the street were filled with spectators, the men (with some smug exceptions) standing with hats in hand, the women either daubing at their eyes with lace handkerchiefs or wearing that blank stoic look you saw on the faces of frontier mothers who had buried their children and with them their ability to shed tears. A thump and a puff of white smoke put the whole thing on record in a tripod camera mounted on a scaffold.

A porter opened the door at the back of the caboose and we transferred the box from the hearse onto a braided oval rug spread on the plank floor between a potbelly stove and the upright desk where the conductor kept his tally.

The day's warmth had given way to chill evening, with a stiff breeze tearing the flames away from the streetlamps. I'd started to sweat during the service, and now my own perspiration swaddled me in a clammy sheet. I felt a cold coming on, one of those that lingered. I'll never know how the old man managed it.

Well, I'd have done it again, curse him; every bit of it. All I am is his doing, the good as well as the bad. And he hadn't wasted time about it, beginning on the very first day.

FIVE

Men not bent on mischief do not under normal circumstances break holes in other people's walls. This court is open to an explanation of your conduct."

I'd always been at a loss to read the Judge's humors. Back in 1876, I had no hope of finding tracks on that ground based on fifteen minutes' acquaintance, and the swill served at Chicago Joe's had swollen my brain so that it was scraping the inside of my skull, which was distraction enough. I couldn't decide whether he was offering me a way out or prolonging my agony.

"It was a question of loyalty, sir." Which was as much of a response as I could muster. It came out like a bow scraping a fiddle. My mouth was dry, with wheel ruts in my tongue.

"'Your Honor.' I shall not remind you again, except in the form of a five-dollar fine for contempt. Mr.—" He riffled the pages on his desk, squinting; his vanity even then was full-grown, to the point of refusing to wear glasses in company. "Marmaduke?"

"Murdock, s—" I swallowed the dust I'd stirred up. "Your Honor."

"To what loyalty do you refer?"

"The Union. Your Honor."

Again he consulted his papers, then pushed them aside. "Since the complaint makes no mention of politics, I shall entertain elucidation."

The word was three syllables past my education, but I took a stab at its definition. "The barman said that no Yankee can hold his liquor well enough to jump over his own hat when placed on the floor. When I took him up on it—wagering ten dollars on the outcome—he snatched my own hat off my head and threw it in a corner. That left me with only one choice, to pick up a chair and knock a hole in a wall."

"Which wall separated the saloon from Chicago Joe's private parlor. The woman is known to this community as a generous contributor. She took up a collection to replace the plain panes in St. Sebastian's Presbyterian Church with stained glass, salting the mine with a hundred dollars' gold from her own safe. As this court sees it, by violating the lady's privacy you profaned the House of God."

That was dangerous ground. I was just off three weeks riding drag on a herd of fleabags, and what the barman was pleased to call Kentucky rye contained enough fusel oil to invite a thumping headache even before the dizzying effect of the spirits had worn off. I was treading water minus the wit to wade no higher than my ankles.

"If I knew the lady's quarters were on the other side, I'd not have done it," I said. "As it was I was acting on behalf of comrades perished at Cold Harbor."

"You served Sherman in Virginia?"

"Rosecranz, Your Honor. Sherman wasn't in command there."

At this point the Judge covered his mouth. To this day I don't know if he was dissembling a grin over my having called his bluff or wrestling with the agony of his unmatched teeth. In any case his face was a mask of doom when he banged his gavel.

"Fifty dollars, half to this court, the other half to Chicago Joe's to cover the repairs."

I had only coppers in my pocket. I'd spent most of my wages before making the bright decision to cap off the day at Joe's. I confessed as much.

"Thirty days." Bang.

His desk wasn't a proper bench, but a former rolltop whose hutch had been removed so that he could stare attorneys and defendants in the eye; the holes were still visible where pegs had held the thing in place. There was then no courthouse, nor yet the promise of one. The rookie jurist dispensed justice from the ground-floor ballroom of a Gothic horror built by an early gold magnate, who had drunk himself to death without making a serious dent in thirty thousand dollars' worth of imported brandy in his cellar. The secret of what had become of the rest was a matter between the Judge and the elected officials who had foreclosed on the estate. Mismatched chairs were arranged in rows to serve as a gallery; not that a drunken brawl attracted as much interest as a gun battle or better, an axe murder. One of the seven locals in attendance coughed dryly and looked at his stem-winder.

The bailiff that year was a gaunt party whose complexion

looked like badly cured macadam. He was conducting me in manacles to the door and the jailhouse beyond when a note came into his hands from an apprentice to the prosecutor. He glanced at the angular script, grunted, and steered me farther up the entrance hall.

Blackthorne's chambers were in a former pantry, paneled in cottonwood and still smelling of potatoes and dried beans. His desk was a plain whitewashed kitchen table, scarred all over with knife cuts. The Judge, standing in his robes, directed the officer to remove my cuffs and dismissed him. Hanging his uniform of office on a scarred coat tree, he said, "Are you aware of the scientific theory that venom can be applied as an antidote to snakebite?"

"Your Honor?"

"You can call me sir in this room. I am suggesting a cure for the after-effects of the evil nectar pressed upon the unsuspecting at Joe's. By thunder, man, hair of the dog!"

"Ah. I've heard something along those lines."

"Next time you patronize the place, bring the wherewithal to secure the fare the proprietress reserves for the local gentry."

Swinging open the door of a six-foot pie safe, he produced a green bottle with a cork sealed in red wax and filled two cutglass tumblers with honey-colored liquid. It smoked a little when exposed to the air.

He set a glass on the far side of the table and sat in a Jefferson swivel with an Indian blanket draped over the back, probably covering tears in the upholstery. He was in his shirtsleeves and waistcoat, his watch chain and Masonic fob glittering in the light of a coal-oil lamp. I pulled up a split-bottom chair at his invitation. He drank, I drank. Right away the fog began to lift and the throbbing receded into the background.

"Your fine has been paid," he said.

"Does that mean I'm free to go?"

"Aren't you the least bit interested in who paid it?"

"That's easy. The only man who hasn't spent everything he earned on the drive is the man who led it. Ford Harper, the owner of the Bar Slash Aitch Ranch."

"He sent a message as well."

"That's just as easy. I'm fired."

"The rest may be more difficult to guess. He gave you a reference. He said he never had a better foreman and that if it weren't for you, there would have been blood spilled between hands he couldn't afford to lose."

"He's a good Christian."

"He added that if you weren't such an insubordinate jackass you'd have gone on being foreman instead of sticking your nose up a cow's ass for sixty miles."

"He's a bastard."

"Ranchers are in general. I'm curious to learn just how you prevented bruised feelings among the men from escalating to tragedy."

"I bruised more than their feelings."

He frowned. His face showed more mobility than it had when court was in session. "If I hadn't seen you in person before he told me of your abilities, I'd have expected a bigger man. You've but a few inches and ten pounds on myself, and I am not regarded as middle size."

"Cowhands don't displace much as a rule. Mustangs won't carry a big man as far as necessary to deliver a herd to market."

"What's your experience with firearms?"

"I found that when I pull on one end, the other end makes noise. I don't own one at the moment."

He leaned back in his chair and swung the pie safe open again. I solved the mystery of the change in his features then: A set of false teeth rested in a pickle jar on a shelf inside. From the next shelf down he slid a revolver and laid it on my side of the table.

I hesitated, then set down my glass and picked up the weapon. It was a slender five-shot self-cocker, chambered for .45, with an octagonal barrel, a curved walnut grip, finely checked, and a brown finish. It bore a strong resemblance to a Colt, but it wasn't a Colt. It had a medium heft and good balance. The cylinder was empty.

"It's an English piece," Blackthorne said, "manufactured by the firm of Deane, Adams, and Deane, originally makers to the late Prince Albert. It came into the possession of this court by way of a gambler I tried last spring. He got into a disagreement with a local teamster, whose Schofield misfired. The Deane-Adams did not.

"That faulty Schofield saved the gambler's life twice," he went on. "The second, when I ruled him not guilty on the grounds of self-defense. I fined him for carrying a firearm inside the city limits, and confiscated the revolver in lieu of a fine. Can you master it?"

"I can't prove it in this room."

"I am not asking you to. Any fool can point and pull a trigger. I'm more interested in a man with the ingenuity to figure out how to leap over a hat set in the angle between two adjacent walls. Incidentally, whatever possessed you to think I'd be swayed by your loyalty to the Union? For all you know I supported the Confederacy."

"You hung a portrait of Lincoln on the wall behind the bench."

"That was Horace Greeley, and it was hanging there when

I arrived. However, your instincts were sound. I am a Republican appointee. My papers were signed by President Johnson, who served as vice president under Lincoln. That little gambit is another reason for my interest in you."

I nodded. "I'm confused. I came into this room prepared to hang my spurs for a month, and now I'm supposed to leave with the gift of a twenty-dollar pistol."

"You won't think it a gift for long. Are you wanted anywhere? I shall find out if you are, so you might as well tell me. I haven't a warrant for anyone of your name or description, so you'll walk out of here a free man regardless."

"No one wants me at present, Harper included."

He drew something between two fingers from a waistcoat pocket and clapped it on the table beside my glass. The scrap of pewter reflected little light. "Pin this on, raise your right hand, and repeat after me."

"Why would I do that?"

"To avoid sentencing to a road gang for vagrancy. You said under oath you have only pennies to your name."

"You said I was a free man."

"I did not. I said if you told me you were wanted, you were free to walk out. I am taking you at your word you are not. I cannot countenance allowing a common tramp to roam the streets of the capital. Such carelessness leads too often to mischief."

He wasn't through. "In addition. You confessed to wagering ten dollars you did not have. That is fraud, punishable by six months in the territorial prison in Deer Lodge. You must agree my leniency in offering thirty days on a gang instead is generous."

The son of a bitch had had that badge in his pocket when

I came in. I didn't think he carried it for luck. I had half a mind to take the offer to bust rocks for the territory instead. More than two decades later I still wondered if I'd have been better off to listen to that half.

SIX

—

Mrs. Blackthorne and I chose seats across the aisle from each other and three rows apart. We had no mutual dislike; it's human nature to stake one's territory with elbow room to spare. She had a basket of yarn in her lap and her hands were a blur as she worked the needles. I'd brought along my Bible, but I'd slept poorly the night before and reading the ancient vocabulary made my eyes smart. I rested my head against the lace slip on the back of the plush Pullman chair and watched the throng waiting on the platform for the train to pull out so they could put mourning behind them and return to work. The view was all bare male heads, red female noses buried in hankies, and the brazen bells of the band's instruments blaring "After the Ball."

The notes were muted, however, battered back by din.

From the direction of the jail continued the racket that had been taking place on and off since the news had come from the courthouse; the inmates awaiting trial or removal to the penitentiary in Deer Lodge rattled their mess tins between the bars of their cells, more or less to the accompaniment of a squeezebox in the inexpert hands of a trusty. There was a mystique connected with just how these men segregated from the community learned about such things as the Judge's death before anyone else in town, but I didn't see anything exotic in it. Reliable as he was when on duty, on his own time bailiff Gottlieb carried a pocket flask full of tongue-loosener, and the turnkey usually assigned to convey defendants between the courthouse and the jail was his brother-in-law.

The melody, what there was of it, was a lively jig. Whether the bastards thought Blackthorne's passing would assist their defense or they were just happy he was worm-ready, I couldn't say. The rattling and wheezing scraped a razor across my nerves. It almost made me miss that tired ballad from the East.

At long last the engineer blasted the whistle twice, the car rocked back, then assumed forward motion. The rows of spectators gathered under the station's porch roof slid toward the rear of the train, and then they were lost in the steam from the jets and the smoke from the stack.

We swung north toward Great Falls, making a stop there for the locals to turn out and another band to play the Judge's favorite air. When the conductor, a young man for the trade—but then I'd lately noticed how much younger the population around me was growing—entered and announced that a man who said he was with the Montana Press Association had requested an interview, I looked at Mrs. Blackthorne, who shook her head vigorously without interrupting her knitting. I said to have the fellow meet me in the caboose.

"Marshal?"

He was standing at the foot of the coffin, a stringy six-footer with an impressive black horsecollar beard. Just looking at his striped suit of clothes, square fawn-colored hat with a narrow crimped brim, and the liquid shine on his boots, I knew he had a neatly knotted cravat and fresh collar hidden under all those whiskers.

"Deputy," I corrected him. "I work for a living."

He changed hands on his fold of foolscap to shake my hand. "Howard Rossleigh. I report directly to the wire service. Are you ready to become famous?"

"I already am. Page Murdock."

His faded blue eyes were polite, but I could tell the name meant nothing; another signatory that I'd begun living past my time. There'd been a period when I couldn't enter a mercantile anywhere on the frontier without seeing an unrecognizable representation of my face and figure on a red-and-yellow cover in a rack.

"I suppose it serves me right for not getting shot in the back before my fortieth birthday," I said. "I'd just as soon you left me out of your story. It isn't my funeral train."

He made some unintelligible marks with an orange pencil stump. "I shall refer to you as 'a source connected with the federal court.'"

"That will do for now."

His brows lifted. "Am I to take that as an indication you plan to retire now that your employer has passed?"

"No. I'm just looking around."

I didn't know if I was more put out by the misapprehension that the marshals' service paid a pension like the railroads and the printers' guild, or that I looked old enough to pack it in and sit whittling in front of a dry goods. Well, I felt old enough. If the clarinet playing outside was pitched any higher it would call in the hogs.

"Is it true Judge Blackthorne hanged sixty-six men?"

"You could say that. You could also say he spared a hundred and thirty-two from the scaffold."

Scribble, scribble. "We in the press are divided between those who considered him a beacon of justice and those who thought him a barbarian who abused his office. How did you see him?"

"Usually by appointment."

It went on in that vein, me turning aside arrows and he showering the caboose with graphite dust. When, stopping two days later in Lewistown, I bought a copy of *The Montana Democrat*, I wasn't much surprised to read that nothing I'd said made the wire column. He'd either found someone more amenable to his purpose or made up a quote referring to the Judge as "a blood-and-thunder throwback to the pioneer past."

I was mollified at least that I'd got shut of the fellow. After all the encounters I'd had with journalists, I should have been prepared for what a festering thorn he'd become.

The widow and I barely spoke while riding in the day coach, but she proved an energetic conversationalist when we sat opposite each other in the dining car. Caspar, the silent cook, had a way with sidemeat and boiled rutabagas that likely was missed at the Last Chance Hotel in his absence, but his coffee would peel the hide off an elephant. We both added liberal amounts of sugar and cream to our brew.

"We differed in entertainment," she said; I'd already noted that she usually referred to her late husband in pronouns only. "He liked acrobats and dancers, while I preferred the legitimate theater. I well remember the row we had when I suggested dragging him to 'East Lynne' for the third time."

"I never heard a cross word between you."

She stirred the sludge in her cup. "Living in Washington,

cheek-by-jowl with the families of other representatives, one learns to keep one's voice low. I can assure you we aired our disagreements; but his quick temper was as swift to spend itself."

That hadn't been my experience. I'd found him short-fused but slow to forgive.

I asked her what her plans were once the Judge was in the ground.

"My sister wired an invitation to move in with her and her husband. He is a lobbyist for the sugar interests in Cuba, where there is talk of our going to war with Spain, so I do not imagine he will much be underfoot. I do not envision it as a permanent arrangement. I'm left with enough to support myself. A small accommodation will serve, and I suppose the drearily rewarding existence of an aged widow engaged in volunteer work."

I'd begun to enjoy her company. A relative crowding in with a married couple, who mentioned the likelihood of her male host being "underfoot," was uncompromising; one who referred to charitable deeds as tedious was just the kind of woman Blackthorne would have chosen to spend most of his life with. The mystery remaining was how he'd come to light upon me for the rest.

Or from the start, had he seen in me the raw material he required, and placed me in the charge of men who knew what he wanted and how to achieve it? God knew he had them to spare, snatched from cells and scaffolds and offered one last chance to turn their talents in a better direction. Was he that devious, or had so short a time and so small a distance away from his actual presence already painted a picture more cold-blooded than the original? In only a few days he had begun to take on the stylized graven outline of something cast in bronze.

SEVEN

———

I'm Cocker Flynn. You can call me Flynn till I say different."

I said, "If you don't like your given name, why not change it?" This happened twenty years in the past. I was still young then and inclined to be curious.

"Already did. Who'd christen his kid Cocker?"

He was a banty rooster, shorter even than Blackthorne, with bow legs, steel splinters in his handlebars, and twice as many knuckles as any man I'd ever met. I figured he hadn't broken them swinging at fence posts. He wore clothes made up of pieces of different suits: checked waistcoat, striped trousers, plain black jacket, all of which may have looked elegant when he first put them on, but his bony knees, barrel-stave ribs, and knobby elbows had gnawed the material almost through, giving strangers a fair idea of how he'd look stripped to his raw red flesh. For some reason he wore a Mexican sombrero with a brim the size of a bicycle wheel. With his short braided frame it turned him into a thumbtack. Not that anyone would say it to his face, because he had something of the hornet about him: sting first, ponder later. I had the luck to witness that part of his character from the sidelines.

His real name, I found out five years later, when it was engraved on a brass plaque dedicated to deputies slain in the service of the court, was Cornelius; the Judge held no truck with aliases on formal occasions. Flynn had been four years with the federals in Kansas, and was among the first wave of peace officers Blackthorne asked to relocate to the territory based on his record. He'd retired undefeated at forty from the bare-knuckle ring, and in Topeka, Hays, and Dodge City had a reputation for drawing his pistol only when his target was out of range of his fists.

Chances are the nickname had come to him by way of his passion for cockfights. In the time I knew him I'd seen him bet a month's wages, earned by dint of sweat and spilled blood, on the outcome of two scrawny birds locked in a struggle to the death.

"I'd not challenge him," Blackthorne had counseled me. "He's killed two men in physical combat, and after two years a third has yet to awaken."

"What's the job?" I asked Flynn, when we met.

He jerked a thumb over his shoulder. He was standing in the street with his back to Belle Crafton's Castle. I was facing him. Like Chicago Joe's Coliseum, it was a toney place with bronze carriage lamps set between windows shrouded in purple swag, beveled-glass double doors, and the name standing out in copper letters across the front. You twisted an engraved oval brass knob next to the doors, a bell rang inside, a rectangular panel embossed with a peacock slid aside, and if your face was familiar or looked respectable enough, you won admission. Belle, it was rumored, had turned away a high-ranking agent of the Bureau of Indian Affairs because his breath stank of trade whiskey.

"One of the girls refused to lay with a drunk miner till he came back from the Cathay Gardens smelling like lilacs instead of prairie-dog shit. He's taken it as an insult and now he's making noise about blowing her spine out through her belly. Got him a Russian forty-four that'd sure enough fill the bill."

"Not prizefighter work."

He blew air through his moustaches—in regret, I thought—and unshipped his sidearm, a stubby Colt .44 with a two-inch barrel, converted from cap-and-ball. It was short enough to carry in the saddle pocket of his coat but heavy enough to make it bag. The worn amber handle leaned out from his hip when undrawn. "I asked for help thinking you could keep him busy while I snuck up behind and rabbit-punched him; but he's gone and set himself up with his back to the wall and the girl tighter to his chest than a good hand of cards."

I fingered the Deane-Adams in my holster. I hadn't had the chance to try it out; which was a step back from confidence going into a desperate situation, and the cause of many an early passing. "I'm not certain I could make a kill-shot that would avoid his twitching."

"I might could give you a piece of a second. Reckon you can manage that?"

Just for reassurance I slid out the weapon, freed the cylinder, and spun it. I don't normally hold with spiritual communication between flesh and mineral, but everything about the action said it would perform as intended. I re-seated it, lifted it again, and let it fall oh so gently into place, hoping for that little air pocket that might keep it from settling in tight for the

winter. The fast-draw was mostly an invention of the romantic pen, but lives had turned on the flick of an eyelash, and to
enter with guns drawn might trigger a maniac into action.

You'll find all this in a manual, probably; written by some
military expert at West Point, who'd never heard a shot fired
outside the range. It doesn't necessarily work in practice.

Hereupon Cocker Flynn, who'd read all these things, in the
tone of my voice and the language of my body, dismasted me
with a wolfish grin.

"Just look to the miner's right eye—that's the target, as he's
right-handed, so's he'll have it cocked away from the girl—jerk
and fire to the line of your vision. It's like swinging an axe; so
long as your keep your eye on the spot to cut, the blade'll hit
it every time."

"When do I fire?"

"Oh, you'll know."

We spread the doors, walked Indian-file down a narrow
corridor, swung open the batwings associated with the trade
(superfluous as they were, they were as endemic as the three
globes above the entrance to every pawnbroker's shop in civilization), and spread out inside the big room with its baize-
topped tables, long mahogany bar, brass rail, and plump
gauze-clad reclining beauties in oils on the walls (along with
the obligatory portraits of Washington and Lincoln in chipped
gilt frames). The peanut shells were in place on the floor, the
reek of beer, whiskey, and tobacco as thick as fug on the third
day at Gettysburg, and the clever signal-devices in place on the
walls; an arrow attached to a screw twisted in the direction of
the name of the hostess whose services were required by the
last customer.

The girls were young, good-looking, and ladylike—up to the
point of negotiation—and would stay that way just as long as

the mines kept paying out. When the shafts went dry, you wouldn't have to ask the sourdoughs to learn the bad news; every dewy-eyed thing in town would be on the stage road to Deadwood or Creede or Tombstone, or wherever the color was still bright, leaving behind the slatterns who were either too worn down to travel or wrinkled and scrawny beyond the ability to pull stake and stand the fare. That was the barometer of success (or failure) in prospecting camps: the comeliness (or lack of it) in their hostesses. You had only to look at them to know whether to stay or move on.

Helena was prospering, if the young woman with the wild eyes was any indication. Her waist, corseted or otherwise, was narrow enough for the customer's arm to encircle it tight, and the only lines in her neck radiated from the muzzle of the barrel-heavy Smith-and-Wesson revolver pressed against it. If he'd truly intended to relocate her spine by way of her belly, he was no student of the human body. But a slug of that size through any vital spot was all that was necessary.

He didn't look like such of a much of a desperado; a fellow in his early twenties, if that, retaining pouches of baby fat in his cheeks, whose fuzz he could scrape off with a thumbnail, a St. Christopher's cross winking from a chain around his neck, and the general look of a kid who'd wandered into something he hadn't prepared for and that offered no way out. I'd seen the same expression in the eyes of a mule too tangled in the muck of the Rocky Fork and too exhausted from the struggle to climb the bank and save itself, and me without a lasso handy. I'd seen the moment when it decided to give up and let go. The aim here was to do something the moment the boy came to the same conclusion and before he acted on it. Until that tiny window opened, he was like a mainspring wound too tight, set to break at the touch of a trigger.

56 LOREN D. ESTLEMAN

We could have saved him, if that was the job. But the whore was the job.

It was the woman's eyes that decided the thing for me. I'd been prepared for a wild stare, the irises surrounded entirely by white, like a spooked horse. But hers were dull, like tarnished coins, as if she'd expected all her life for her curtain to close in just such a circumstance as this. She wore the hem of her skirt hitched up on one side, a local advertising tradition, exposing a band of white flesh above her garter, which in the manhandling had let loose of her black stocking; it crumpled at the knee like a snakeskin in mid-slough. But after all these years I remember most that look of numb resignation on her face. However this thing came out, whatever new horror came along to end her existence, whatever happened here, was at best nothing more than a delay of the inevitable.

"Look to his eye," Flynn said beneath his breath; beneath it, literally. We were so close I could almost hear his unspoken thoughts. The blood surging through his arteries was like a cataract pouring over a near hill.

As there was just one eye visible, that seemed simple enough; although I didn't know what I was supposed to look for in it. A glint of intention? An instant of weakness? There wasn't time or the means of expression necessary.

"One step more, you sonsabitches!" The muzzle of his weapon pressed deeper into her flesh, constricting her windpipe. The wheeze of short-drawn breath that followed might have been a leak in a gas pipe.

Flynn wasn't a man for words. Aiming from the hip he pressed the trigger of the squat-barreled Colt and shot the woman through her exposed thigh. The bullet entered the pale flesh two fingers directly above the rosette that decorated the garter.

She folded, as anyone would with a slug fired through a limb at a distance of no more than eight feet. Blood left the wound in a high bright arc and splatted the tessellated floor.

In that instant I had a four-foot field of vision, broad enough to punch a hole through a window shutter anywhere I pleased; but the miner's eye was my target of direction. The Deane-Adams' front sight was set solid.

His left eye starred red. A piece of his skull struck the wall behind him with the sound of a poker chip falling to the floor. His finger tensed on the trigger, not strong enough to work the hammer. He fell in a sort of spiral, his knees twisting left, his torso twisting right, and sort of screwed himself to the floor, making no more noise than a load of wet laundry landing at the bottom of a chute; his arms tensed briefly, as if trying to push himself upright, but not enough to raise the weight of his body far enough to show daylight. He settled to the floor like wet mortar between the forms.

His S&W Russian had fallen a few inches away from his hand, which continued to twitch. I kicked it out of his reach while Flynn drew his bandanna from around his neck and twisted it around the woman's thigh above the wound, staunching the gush of blood. The flesh looked doughy. It excited no more lust than tallow.

As he worked he spoke. "Lost two telling 'em to duck. They was both struck like statues and I lost 'em. Bullet makes the decision for 'em."

"Then you've worked this before." I was breathing shallowly; the English pistol hung at the end of my arm heavy as a broadaxe.

"Couple of times. This the first one on the end of a bastard's gun come through alive."

"He's the first one I ever killed."

He glanced up from his labors, his eyes as flat as stove lids.
"I heard you fit in the war."

"It isn't the same thing."

"That's gospel. Them rebs was defending their home and
you kilt 'em for it. Just now you saved a life, such as it is.
Killing's like snowflakes. No two are the same." He grinned,
baring only his lower teeth. "Good shooting, yonker. Welcome
to Blackthorne's court."

EIGHT

The cold I'd been expecting ever since the Judge lay in state had arrived bang on time the first night of the trip. I lay down in my berth in my coffin-like compartment with a trickle in my throat and awoke to find my head packed tight with mortar. I spent an hour turning this way and that to clear the pipes, breathing through my mouth and sanding my gullet even rawer, then dressed and went to the dining car to sit. Caspar, the mute cook, was slumped on a stool behind the counter, half-dozing; which as the days rolled past I suspected was the closest he came to sleeping at all. He sprang from his station lugging coffee equipment, and filled a cup with lava from a blue enamel pot; the rising steam cleared my passages like a Turkish bath, but only so long as it took to cauterize my throat with the scalding brew and return the cup to its saucer. I'd wound a bandanna around my neck to catch cinders before they dived down inside my collar. I yanked it loose and blew my nose into it with a honk and a rattle.

Caspar grinned. I had him down for one of those who drew cheer from the afflictions of others, but when he was back behind the counter he poured hot water from a pan into a glass tumbler with a thick bottom, spooned in at least a cup and a half of soggy buckshot that was probably actually blackstrap molasses, shook in coarse black pepper, lots of it, added a pearl onion, cut a lemon in two using a knife with a wicked-looking triangular blade, and squeezed both halves to a pulp in his fist over the brew, squirting in juice. He cranked open a can of sardines and with a flourish fed two into the glass by their tails, then churned the mess with a mixer, turning the handle briskly until the liquid assumed a gray liverwurst shade. He brought the glass to my table, trailing steam like smoke from a stack.

When it was in front of me I stared at it with my palms flat on either side, as if he'd deposited a diamondback on the table and one twitch of a muscle would make it strike. He made a dumb show, pinching his nostrils between thumb and forefinger, tipping back his head, and raising a cupped hand to his mouth. He held it there for thirty seconds at least, working his throat the whole time. I was to gulp it all down without stopping.

I didn't trust him or the drink, but my head was blocked again and just the thought of taking in air past the scraped and blistered lining of my windpipe made death by poison seem not so bad a fate. I'd eaten dog served by Cheyenne renegades, son-of-a-bitch stew in a mining camp where Gila monsters were the only four-footed game in forty miles, and was still here to review the bill of fare. I pinched my nostrils and tipped back my head. I felt the damn fool I knew I looked like.

I took a deep breath, let it out, breathing iron shavings both ways, and poured the stuff down in a thin trickle, swallowing the glutinous mass of coagulated sugar, sharp onion, bitter lemon, suffocating pepper, greasy fish, and simmering water; it went gloop-gloop-gloop, like pouring axle grease. I nearly choked, but I got it all down in one long draught, slow as a load of anvils moving up a long grade. Caspar, knowing what was coming, withdrew a couple of yards down the aisle. I almost made it to the bottom before it changed its mind and backed up into my nose. I shot forward, coughing and spraying molten lead through every orifice in my face.

Instinct cut in. I had the Deane-Adams half out of its holster when my head began to clear, holes opening in the dam as if bored by a swarm of carpenter bees; I heard little bells tinkling. I let the revolver slip back into place and sat back, sucking in great gusts of sweet air. It hadn't tasted so good since the time someone cut me free of a noose back in '80.

I blew my nose again, checked the bandanna for blood, found none, and looked up at the cook with new eyes. "You ought to bottle this stuff. You'd never have to fry another egg."

He rolled his scrawny shoulders and tapped the pocket of his chef's tunic where his watch chain came to an end. I didn't know what he was about until I woke up at dawn with my skull heavier than it had been the night before. Caspar's miracle cure lasted only till gravity took over. I figured I'd let the disease run its course without any more interference.

In Miles City, among yet another crowd listening to yet another band playing "After the Ball"—this time more elaborately, with a second violinist and a saxophone contributing at least a variation on the usual dirge—I spotted a familiar face and beard. How Howard Rossleigh of the Montana Press Association had beaten an express train to the station became clear when he explained that he'd been engaged by W. R. Hearst of *The New York Journal* to cover the Judge's last journey, and provided with a small fast former yard engine and advance telegrams to extinguish every red lantern in its path. Rechristened *The Javelin*, the train burned anthracite coal, which went farther than wood and made unnecessary frequent stops to restock the tender.

I said, "I knew readers of the Eastern press ate up the Judge like licorice whips, but he isn't any more likely to grant interviews now than when he was still kicking."

"It isn't Blackthorne Mr. Hearst is interested in," Rossleigh said. "It's you."

Casting about for a hook, the publisher had lit upon me: The loyal minion, faithful all the way to the cemetery.

A special train and the favors a man needed to call in to arrange the cooperation of the railroads seemed like a lot of expense and bother to go to over one broken-down deputy; but Hearst had more dollars than sense and had declared war on all his competitors. In two years he'd manufacture a genuine war with Spain, practically on his own, with no end but to attract more readers. No one knew it then, but that would be the end of the West except in history books. Who cared to follow the adventures of dusty saddle tramps now that all the Indians were penned up, the frontier shut down, and men charging up a hill in Cuba led by a bookworm with his eye on Washington?

I nearly gave Rossleigh the boot there and then. It would have been easy; the caboose's rear door was open and he stood with his back to it. But I'd had experience enough of reporters to know he'd probably double back and pester Mrs. Blackthorne for details about the bashful civil servant, so I told him some stretchers, borrowing adventures from such as Cocker

Flynn, Doc Miller, and the bloody Brothers Mercy as well as the kind of claptrap Buffalo Bill spun for the rubbernecks who paid to see his extravaganza. Facing a couple of dozen veteran gunmen with only five cartridges in my sidearm, plowing hostile Indians under the hooves of my mighty steed, and capturing Cole Younger, William Bonney, and Clay Allison unassisted was sure to tip him to the truth and make him give up on me. He scribbled on another of his folds of foolscap, using what I thought was the same orange pencil stub, shorter now but with its attached eraser intact; journalists seldom edit their notes. But he wasn't writing constantly. Most likely he was registering his impressions rather than setting down my jabber. I approved. My strategy was working.

I thought.

When we pulled into Glendive I saw a fair likeness of myself in the lead column of *The Montana Post* (Rossleigh either doubled as an illustrator or had given one a decent description; though I didn't know I looked quite so mean) and an account of my interview with most of the balderdash left out and bales of florid prose dumped in about my undying devotion to the Judge's memory. I'd been demoted from a riproaring frontier Galahad to the old dog refusing to desert its master's grave.

It was more of Erasmus Callaway's mechanizations. If I had any doubt about that, it evaporated when he was quoted three times in the article. He'd wring all the attention he could out of Blackthorne's corpse as thoroughly as Caspar squeezed his lemons. It would pay off, at least for a while. Although he would lose out for governor later that year, the race was close enough for Callaway's name to come up when the Republican brass was considering a running mate for William McKinley. More cautious heads seized upon the bookworm from Cuba, who

was a political firebrand, in order to maneuver so dangerous
a character into an office that was considered a backwater
(a ploy that would backfire in a Buffalo, New York, train station on September 13, 1901).

I crossed the line into North Dakota with a bellyful of coffee and a dollop of brandy from a medicinal bottle in one of
Caspar's cupboards and the shadow of a beginning of hope for
recovery. I hadn't visited the place since before it was parti-
tioned off from South Dakota at statehood time. In those
charged days following Custer's slip at the Little Big Horn, it
was a different place, with a throttled-up brave showing up at
every turn like a prairie dog hole, but it looked as bleak as ever,
gridiron-flat with wind soughing through waist-high grass
when we laid over and waving past mile upon mile when we
resumed. It was mesmeric, blurring the vision like yellowed
memories.

NINE

"What you reading, Page Murdock?"

Asking the question, the young Cheyenne pasted a sneer to his well-set features, as if he thought curiosity a sign of weakness.

I didn't challenge him, as I was his guest; we both avoided the term *prisoner*, which might pitch our relationship into even more dangerous territory than it was. The year was 1878, and dangerous enough for anyone living in Indian country.

I marked my place with a finger and closed the book; not that I needed to look at its tooled-leather cover to remind myself of its title. In my short time in the Dakota Territory village I'd learned the uniquely Indian habit of circling twice around a subject before addressing it.

"*Spenser*. Published in Philadelphia in 1860."

"Spenser, he is the hero?"

"He's dead. While he lived he was a poet." I tipped it back open to the page I'd marked and read:

> *Rehearse to me, ye sacred sisters nine,*
> *The golden brood of great Apolloes wit,*
> *Which late you powred forth as ye did sit*
> *Beside the silver springs of Helicone,*
> *Making your musick of hart-braking mone!"*

"What it mean?"

Ghost Shirt—which was the name he took when he splintered off from the Cheyenne nation to lead a massacre, and before he broke loose of the federal penitentiary—was a poser. Like most of the white gunmen who drifted from mining camp to cattle town to border village, he'd read all the popular novels—in his case in mission school, where the agent in charge bought them by the bushel for pennies and charged the Bureau of Indian Affairs for Shakespeare—and had learned how to behave and talk like the stoic braves of Buntline, Ingraham, and the rest of the army of poetasters who'd flooded the stalls with Mother Goose tales dressed up with war paint and scalpings. His grammar was at least as good as mine. It had been hammered into him with a straightedge across his knuckles. Whether he preferred pidgin English in imitation of those paper warriors or as some kind of private joke against white oppressors, I could never decide. And he always addressed me using my full name.

"God only knows. I know he couldn't spell. The man I work for lent it to me with some other books to teach me to talk like an educated man instead of a muley cowhand."

"Why?"

"He says he doesn't want his marshals to embarrass him in public, but he's had men on the job longer than me who make a Chinese bootblack sound like a St. Louis banker. They all take work on the side as saloon bouncers and tax collectors for the county sheriff, though, so I expect he can't stand to see a man draw pay between assignments doing nothing but sitting on his butt."

Ghost Shirt, who was crouching on the other side of the fire in the lodge he'd had set aside for me, barked a short laugh, leaned over, pulled aside his breechclout, and smacked his own backside. It sounded like a muleskinner's whip. I had to laugh too. It was the first moment of human warmth that had passed between us since I'd stumbled into his dog soldiers while tracking him. One week later, he was dead, wearing the manacles I'd put on his wrists.

A steel wheel hit an uneven joint in the tracks with a bang, shaking me out of my doze. The sleep that had eluded me in my berth had come back to claim me next day in the chair car. I'd slept too many years on cornshucks in ricks, ground pounded into granite by buffalo, and trees next to puddles that manufactured mosquitoes the way Detroit produced stoves, to find peace on mattresses stuffed with down; yet another legacy the Judge had left me.

The dream was pretty much the way it had happened, so far as I could piece it back together after nearly twenty years. I hadn't thought about Ghost Shirt and his attempt to rally the High Plains tribes in a suicidal last-ditch assault on the white man. It was being back in North Dakota—just northern Dakota then, before the territory was cloven in two for purposes of management when it won its star on Old Glory—that brought it all back. I swore I'd never return. Blackthorne wouldn't have forgotten that pledge when he settled upon me to escort his shell back to carpetbagger country.

I finished the reading program he'd assigned me by the end of my second year with the court: the bulk of Spenser, everything available to that point from Robert Browning (the Judge had warned me against Elizabeth Barrett's "insipid bleating"), Darwin, Burton, some of Clemens, all of Homer, and Shakespeare, who I came to appreciate when I started reading the lines aloud and that way found the trail he broke. I preferred the tragedies to the comedies, with the exception of *The Taming of the Shrew*, which I remembered years later when I met a woman who might have modeled for the title character. Much of it was like slogging through ropy camptown mud, slipping every third step; some of it was padlocked tight against me and my kind. I never could find tracks in Ralph Waldo Emerson, for instance; but I learned not to say "ain't" in every conversation, and—more important—when to say it and to who. Whom. It's come in handy setting down these memories for someone to find in my old army footlocker when I'm in the ground.

The widow sat farther up the aisle in her backward-facing seat, contributing to her knitting at a rate slightly faster than we were moving across flat unobstructed prairie. What seemed to have started as a muffler was rapidly approaching a lap robe. The young conductor entered the car from the direction of the caboose, trailing a scent of apple-flavored pipe smoke and straight gin and carrying a yellow Western Union envelope. The train must have made a stop while I was asleep; that troubled me, as I'd depended on my instincts to alert me to any change no matter how deep I was under. Of all the enemies that would kill me, the odds were steadily improving in the favor of age.

Mrs. Blackthorne looked up at the man touching the visor of his cap, set aside her basket, and accepted the envelope. She tore open the flap with a thumb and adjusted her spectacles to read the flimsy. She shook her head at the conductor, who had evidently asked if she wanted to reply at the next stop. When he came back toward the exit, she caught my eye and waved the unfolded paper her direction.

She handed me the wire as soon as I was in reach.

MRS BLACKTHORNE
CONDOLENCES ON YOUR GREAT LOSS
STOP IF YOUR ITINERARY ALLOWS PLEASE
SEE ME IN SAINT PAUL STOP ADDRESS TO
FOLLOW
                    NIGEL MORTON ESQ
        MORTON WINSLOW AND MORTON
                    ATTYS AT LAW

"Do you know Morton?" I gave it back.

She shook her head. "Nor Winslow either. Do you suppose they have some legal grudge against Harlan?"

"They wouldn't be the first. Will you go?"

"If you will accompany me."

"I'm sure that's what the Judge would advise."

"Now is as good a time as any to stop asking what he would advise and start relying on myself."

"If you don't want to, don't go."

She glared at me over the tops of her octagonal lenses. "When was the last time you did not do something because you did not want to?"

"That would be the first day I set eyes on Helena."

I returned to my seat. *My* seat; it didn't strike me until then that I'd been sitting in the same one all along, as if it had been assigned to me by a headmaster. On the instant I got restless. I started to rise when the conductor returned, stopping at my seat this time to bend down, turn his back partly toward where Mrs. Blackthorne had resumed knitting, and speak in a murmur. "Would you come with me, sir?"

I studied him. Conductors were as a rule burly men, built to eject unpaid passengers. He was more wiry than stout, his head attached as by a peg to a tall narrow frame. The mouth was too broad for that face; if he were to open it wide, the top half of his skull might tip over backwards like the top of an apothecary jar.

He seemed to be vibrating with excitation. For an instant I wondered if the Judge had kicked off his covers. Nodding, I stepped into the aisle and followed him through the door at the rear of the car, the largely wasted space in the sleeper, and on into the caboose, where the absurdly unprepossessing box lay as it had, at a shallow angle on the braided rug and the lid nailed shut. The car, always the steadiest regardless of the train, clung tightly to the rails, swaying but little and making only tiny ripples in the ink in the well of the rolltop desk.

"See the door, sir." He pointed unnecessarily; with the door we'd just come through at our backs, the one at the rear was the only one visible.

At first I saw only a door. Then the train rattled over a joint and daylight appeared at the edge opposite the hinges, disappearing again as the door jostled back into its frame.

"I keep it bolted when we're in motion," the conductor said. "I made sure it was bolted after the messenger delivered a wire for Mrs. Blackthorne in Stanton. When I got back from the day coach, the bolt was drawn."

"Could a movement of the train jar it from the socket?"

"Shoot it yourself and see if it could."

I stepped around the coffin, took hold of the bolt, heavy brass almost as big around as my thumb, by the knob and slid it into the tube, brass also, screwed to the door frame. It was fitted tight to the recess and moved stiffly, like the bolt on a single-shot rifle, slamming home with a sharp click. There was some give in the frame; a knife in a determined hand might have moved the bolt from the outside.

"Could anyone have boarded when the train was back in motion?"

"I went to deliver the telegram as soon as we started. We were probably doing about fifteen then. It's possible; but he couldn't have gotten past me once I was in the coach. Tramps!" he spat. "They've gotten bolder since the Panic. Used to be they contented themselves to riding the rods; now they're staking out parlor cars like the gentry."

"Maybe." I turned away from the door and drew the Deane-Adams. "We'll check the sleeper."

The conductor slid a steel coupling-pin from a rack bolted to the wall of the caboose, slapped the end against the palm of his free hand, making a satisfying smack, and pointed it toward the door leading to the adjoining car, indicating I should take the lead. In that moment he took on a few more years in my estimation.

I took the upper berths, he the lower. I grasped the partitions in one hand, prising myself up with a foot on the bottom bunks and sweeping aside the curtains with the barrel of the revolver, while the conductor did the same below with his coupling-pin.

It was monotonous work, and the greatest danger was boredom and complacency. The more empty berths a man encountered, the more he thought chances of finding anyone hiding in one were remote; whereas the opposite was true. But we got from one end of the car to the other, both sides, with nothing to show for our vigilance but a spider riding the rails without a ticket. The conductor put that to rest by squashing it against the birch with the end of his pin.

I alit from the last upper and waited for him to straighten from his stoop across the aisle. "Could he have jumped off?"

The conductor frowned, the muscular movement drawing the ends of his comical moustaches nearly together. "We slowed for the grade. He might have swung off then. I guess he took fright of discovery. The bastards are a lot tougher with each other than with us shacks."

"If he were that timid, why didn't he stick to the rods instead of coming inside?"

"Who can say how this rot thinks? If they had brains they'd make a living instead of stealing rides from the N.P."

"We have to ask what the point was of boarding us in the first place," I said.

"I'm open to suggestions."

"Testing, maybe." I touched the sight of the revolver to my lip, then spun it back into leather. "We won't bother Mrs. Blackthorne with this. Let me know if anything else takes your interest."

TEN

After the ball is over;
after the break of morn,
After the dancers' leaving,
After the stars are gone . . .

The Bismarck Volunteer Fire Brigade contributed strings to its performance, two fiddles and a bass viol that squatted on the platform looking like a pregnant sow. Before that I didn't think the song could sound more insipid. The station was new since I'd visited last, but the city beyond looked the same, apart from the addition of more brick buildings among the frame, strategically placed to create firebreaks. The traffic was still predominantly waterborne: A floating second city made of shallow-draught stern- and sidewheelers stuck their stacks up against the horizon, staining the underside of clouds black with smoke. A whistle blew, sounding like a croupy rooster; a brazen bell rang.

I got my first glimpse of Hearst's *Javelin* parked on a siding. Its name was painted, in gilt Olde-English letters like the masthead of *The New York Journal*, along the entire side of the train. The little switch engine and the train itself looked runty compared to ours. It consisted of one car besides the tender and caboose, a private coach from the look of it, albeit not as ornate as some I'd seen; the Pullman company was democratic, catering to millionaires at every level. I spotted the reporter standing in a small crowd of scribblers from my position in the vestibule of the dining car. He was the only one of the vultures who'd bothered to uncover his head throughout the serenade. He was also the only one not taking notes. Our eyes met, and I had the unsettling feeling his were probing behind mine all the way to the brain.

As the band neared the song's maudlin finish, I squared my shoulders. Part of my unspoken responsibilities was to spare the widow the ordeal of facing the newspapers; and while the closest I'd come to politics was when I cast my first vote for Abraham Lincoln, the trip East had made me a fair hand at directing a press conference. I was about to step down to the platform when a ripple stirred through the straw- and bowler-hatted throng and a bell-shaped figure in black made use of the stepping-stool brought by a porter, with the young conductor supporting her by an elbow.

The wind, a Dakota staple, stirred her heavy veil and warped the verbal exchanges so I caught only snatches of the questions and responses, but I pieced together the rest:

"What sort of husband was he?"

"Having no other husband to compare him with, I could not say."

"Did you attend many hangings?"

"None; nor did he invite me to any. We lived our marital life apart from the court."

"Did you approve of the severity of his decisions?"

"I disapproved just once . . ."

The scribblers leaned forward on the balls of their feet, pencils cocked.

". . . when he allowed the installers to hang the wrong curtains in our parlor."

Grumbles accompanied the scratching of graphite. Rossleigh alone grinned in his beard.

I shouldn't have been surprised at how well she comported herself, although I would have had I not spent as much time with her as I had since the night of the Judge's vigil. She was no hothouse flower, sheltered from the unlovely details of meting out justice on the frontier, but a thorny growth on her own, more than capable of defending her mate's memory by denying trespass upon it. And I'd had experience sufficient of women existing in a place where the men outnumbered them twenty to one. Some withered for lack of gentleness and the companionship of others of their gender, others fled back to the gaslights of the East. Of the rest, many stuck and grew more bitter by the day, the week, the month, the year, until there wasn't a dime's worth of difference between them and their grim partners; as many more assumed bright plumage and lived off the pent-up lust of cowhands, prospectors, teamsters, and highwaymen, for as long as their looks and their health held up. The more stubborn ones dressed and cussed and worked like men and kept their secret to the grave—or the first spill that put them in a doctor's care with their clothes off; they found their own notoriety between red-and-yellow paper covers of the nickel novels.

The tiniest percentage kept its womanness, met men on their level, and either came out ahead or broke even. Beatrice Blackthorne was one of those. What were the odds that I'd have known yet another?

The experience was fresh, and stung like a running sore.

"It's routine," the Judge had said. "But you know how far you can trust that."

We didn't know then, but it would be my last assignment for his court, a prisoner pickup that had gone south faster than the usual; before I got there, in fact. An army deserter who'd doubled back to bushwhack his Sioux tracker had fled west with California in mind, but had gotten only as far as Vinegar Hill, Idaho, where he got into a fight with a waiter who refused to serve him liquor in a restaurant. The waiter gave as good as he got; sent silly by a wicked left, the deserter knocked over a lamp on a table and set fire to a beard growing on the face of an elder from the Mormon community in Lemhi County. By rights the waiter was responsible for the arson, but that side of the street was dry by local ordinance and the founders were almost as serious about temperance as they were about fire. The local law recognized the belligerent from readers; however, the same voters who'd backed selective prohibition had vetoed a tax hike to build a jail, so he was locked in a tool shed pending a response to a wire to Helena.

I figured out later I was just over halfway there by rail when the killer got loose. Using a discarded plank, he dug himself out of the shed by way of the dirt floor and encountered the owner, who picked up a potato fork the officers had removed from inside as a precaution and leaned against the back wall.

The escapee charged him, swinging the plank; but the fork was eleven inches longer. I found my man still waiting for me stretched out on a patch of burnt-out buffalo grass. No one had found the ambition to jerk free the fork, so it was still sticking up from his chest. Leaning over to compare his features to the description in the reader I hit my head on the handle, which did nothing for my temperament. In cases where local authority declined the expense of burying a federal fugitive, Blackthorne held his deputies responsible.

Which was one of the reasons, when I got back home, I intended to stick him with the full treatment at the King Alexander barbershop. We all know how that came out.

So the trip wouldn't be a total loss I booked a room in the Coeur d'Alene Hotel and ordered a steak and a bottle in the restaurant. The meat came burned to a crisp and a goldfish could have swum in the bottle without getting woozy. I was calculating the odds on the coconut cream pie when I spotted an old acquaintance dining alone in a dim corner.

She'd aged; we all had, but there were purple thumbprints under her eyes, she'd wound a telltale scarf around a neck I remembered as long and flawless, and her auburn hair had a brassy tint unconvincing even in the weak glow of the lamp on the table. I brought over the bottle and my glass and said: "Maybe between the two of us we can find out how to raise a ruckus from this mountain runoff. How have you been, Colleen?"

She went on stirring a shallow bowl of consommé with bits of green floating in it for a moment, then looked up. I saw recognition and no surprise. "Page." There was a pause, then she inclined her forehead—it at least was unlined—toward the vacant chair opposite.

I sat, gestured with the bottle. She looked at it, staring as if trying to make out what it was; shook her head. A dyed ten-dril came loose from her chignon and drifted in the current of air in the room like tassel on an ear of corn. "I need a rock just to hold down what's in this bowl. But don't stand on cer-emony. Neither of us ever did, as I recall."

She was dressed as well as ever, in a starched shirtwaist closed at the throat with a cameo pin that peeped out around the fringe of her scarf when she tossed her head to tame the stray lock. It floated free for a moment, then slid back down into the eddy.

"It's been a season," I said. "Where was it, Utah?"

"I can't say. They all run together. I was dealing faro, I re-member that."

"You never did learn to deal square."

"The owner of the saloon didn't care. He set me up under a Chesterfield lamp so I'd be the first thing a customer saw when he came in."

"Not like today."

She glanced at the flimsy flame in the chimney, showing a brief flash of teeth in a smile bitter as sulfur. "The light isn't as kind to me as it used to be. I'm poorly, but I don't expect it to last."

"Is that what the doctor said?"

"I shopped around until I found one that would; that's what brought me to this wide spot in the road. I expect he meant I'd be under worse than the weather by Christmas." She shipped a spoonful and blew on it. There wasn't a bit of steam rising from the soup. "It isn't *that*," she said; although she wasn't looking at the expression on my face. "I was always careful about that, at least. Too many smoky rooms, not enough blood in the alcohol system, too much faith in chance."

She let the spoon drop back into the bowl without tasting

it and looked up again. In that moment I saw a flash of the Colleen Bower I knew, the old sureness just shy of arrogance; but it was as artificial as the coloring in her hair. "I've always been lucky, Page, you know that: cards, risk, survival. I should have laid off more, stored it up. Luck's like water, it runs out. You have to sip it so there's some left when you need it most."

"There's nothing can be done?"

"Short of dealing from a fresh deck?" She shook her head, smiling with her lips tight.

She'd done me dirt so many times I'd lost count, but I'd always come back for more, and I was far from alone. She'd been making her own way in the world since she was in pinafores. Wild Bill—Indian scout, bullwhacker, outlaw, lawman, whatever direction the wind was blowing from—had had nothing on her, without her ever raising so much as a callus on her slender white palms. I filled my glass to the rim and slung it back as I hadn't in years. There was just enough busthead to burn my stomach; not enough to climb higher than my rib cage. Not near enough to my head to do me a service. I felt hollow.

"That's what's new with me," she said. "Are you still carrying tin for that bastard in Montana?"

"I'm still riding for Blackthorne's court." I didn't know then he was living out his last hours, but it wouldn't have made any difference. I'd lived past the point where it amused me to gripe about the man who paid my way.

"Haven't you ever wanted to do something else?"

"Every day since I signed on."

In the little silence the hum of conversation and clicking of utensils was as loud as pounding surf. Then she placed both her palms on the table. The impression was she'd need all the strength in both her arms to push herself upright. "I've been saving a bottle of Old Gideon. It's up in my room. Just leave me enough to take the edge off and we'll see if we can work up some of the old ground." Her expression changed, to one I'd never seen on her face. It was fear, but not of death. "That is, if you're not too particular."

"Only about one thing." I rose and offered her a hand up.

Too much train travel had fostered bad habits. I was coddling regrets like the old man I was getting to be. Before long I'd be one of those maudlin wretches you saw on benches streaming tears into their laps. I got up and went back to look in on the Judge. I'd been doing it so long there was no tapering off.

An icy blow off the mountains, combined with the wind of our passage, stiffened my face when I stepped onto the vestibule of the caboose. I knocked twice. When the conductor didn't open up I grasped the handle. The door was unlocked. I stepped inside. I was alone with the pine box. Turning to go, my foot slipped on something. I stepped back and looked at a smear of blood on the floor.

II

DEEPER TOWARD DAWN

ELEVEN

———

I looked from the crimson smudge to the cord that ran the
length of the car below the roof, which activated the
Westinghouse brakes. My hand was halfway to it before I
looked back down at the floor. It wasn't much blood; the conductor might have just nicked himself and gone looking for a
bandage. Most chefs kept simple medical supplies handy. His
first destination would be the dining car. There was no reason to bring the train to a screeching halt over what might be
a cut finger.

To be cautious, I drew my revolver in the sleeper and
checked all the berths. This took no more time than when the
conductor and I had made the same search earlier; we'd left
the curtains spread. Nothing in there but stripped beds—
except those used by the train's tiny manifest of passengers—
the smell of rosewood, and soot on the windows.

Mrs. Blackthorne was in the dining car, drinking tea and

nibbling a cornbread biscuit. The buttery smell was fresh. She'd said that of the two chefs under consideration for the trip, Caspar was the better baker. The homey atmosphere made the drawn gun seem ludicrous. I scabbarded it, but not before the man behind the counter spotted it; not that by expression (and certainly not by word) the weapon meant anything more to him than the crusty spill he was scrubbing at on his griddle.

I leaned across the counter and asked him in a low voice if he'd seen the conductor lately. Out the corner of my eye, I watched the widow dividing her concentration between her light meal and the small clothbound volume she had spread on the table with splayed fingers. It appeared to be a book of household hints; evidently she was preparing for a more modest style of living.

Lips pursed, Caspar directed his attention to the concave ceiling, then shook his head.

"Not to ask for a bandage or sticking-plaster?"

He shook his head again, this time widening his eyes slightly.

"Have you been here all day?"

He glanced toward the water closet. I nodded and left him.

The woman looked up from her book as I approached. "Mr. Murdock, have you given any more thought to that odd telegram?"

I'd forgotten all about it; but I said, "There didn't seem to be much point until you've met with this Morton and find out what it's about."

"Hum. I don't like asking questions I don't know the answers to."

She sounded just like the Judge, right down to the "Hum." I made my tone casual. "Have you seen the conductor in the last half hour or so?" Much longer and the patch of blood would have begun to dry.

"No; but he might have passed while I was reading and I didn't take note. Is it something about the train? It's awfully slow going up these mountains."

"I don't know how the farmers here manage to grow so many potatoes without falling off their patch."

"That's not what I asked."

"Nothing important. I just wondered if he expects us to be across the border before sundown. It's been a long time since I was in Minnesota. I'd hate to miss it in the dark."

"I should have thought your wanderlust a thing past."

"Maybe I'm just restless."

"All the more reason to sit with me for a few minutes. Harlan didn't place a time schedule on this mission."

I couldn't beg off without alerting her to a situation that might not have been dangerous; if so, there was no point in causing alarm. I slid into the seat opposite, drawing the Deane-Adams under the table. Fortunately she was facing the rear of the train, allowing me to face front. The caboose and sleeper car were deserted, and there was no place to hide in the dining car. If trouble came it would be from the direction of the day coach.

"Are you hungry? Caspar is the only man I've ever known who is handy with cornbread. I believe he was raised by a widowed mother with a chronic condition of some kind. Of course, communication with him is challenging."

"No, thank you." It was true we were moving slowly, laboring up a long steep grade, giving an uninvited passenger the opportunity to step off. His complaint may have been with the conductor only. But I couldn't count on either possibility. A grudge against a private citizen is best carried out where an armed lawman isn't present, and coincidence is no match for instinct. I'd never gone wrong assuming the worst was about to happen.

"Have you given any thought to what you'll do with the rest of your life?" she asked; then, hastily, "Of course, I don't mean to suggest that you are leaving the marshals' service, but . . ." She bit into a flaky yellow slice, as if that were the direction of her commentary.

"It's a young man's game, ma'am. I had a friend who said luck has limits. As I see it, I've been traveling on borrowed steam since forty." I shook my head. "The answer to both your questions is no. I'm leaving the court, but I've no idea for what."

She watched me in that same way Blackthorne used to, like a cat crouched on a fence post waiting for a chipmunk to stir from its hole. Whether they'd had so much in common before they wed, or had been married long enough to take on each other's qualities, was fodder for someone with better education.

I gripped the handle of the revolver hard enough to crack it. It wasn't the pressure of the interrogation; I was pretending to concentrate my attention on her face while taking in the length of the car between her and the door behind her.

"You are a Christian, are you not?" she said.

She shifted subjects instantly, the way Blackthorne had done, but in his case it was his courtroom training.

"I am."

"Tomorrow is the Lord's day. Is there a Presbyterian church where we are going?"

"Minneapolis, maybe. It's a good-size town, I hear. But we won't be there in time for services."

"Someplace closer, then. So long as the church is Christian, and so long as it isn't Methodist. I would sooner it be even Catholic. Would you accompany me?"

"It would be my pleasure." I contemplated the antipathy to Methodists among the God-fearing community. They were the Jews of the faith. I'd preached Unitarian in New Mexico Territory during a robbery investigation, rediscovering my interest in the immortal soul while finding tolerance for every path to Paradise. Why there should be so much dissension between people who studied the same Testament mystified me.

I excused myself, putting on an abashed face as if I needed the water closet; remembering to holster my weapon before I slid off the seat. She returned to her reading, and I to my search.

TWELVE

—

The coach was a Pullman parlor, paneled in inlaid mahogany, the windows swagged, the seats upholstered in plush red velvet, and carpeted deeply enough to pull the boot off your foot; the steel wheels clicking over the joints and the steam whooshing from the jets might have been going on in a daydream. Cigar-shaped as it was, the apartment on wheels was a collection of alcoves and shadows, as tempting a place for hide-and-seek as a Queen Anne mansion. A herd of teamsters could have ridden there undetected so long as they stayed put.

I shut the door behind me as quietly as possible, even though anyone crouching in the silence would have heard the rattle and creak of the other cars the moment I'd opened it, and stood for a moment, straining my ears and also my nose; the drawing of a breath, the smell of fresh sweat, the bitter-iron

stench of blood, the residue of tobacco smoked or chewed
would have assured me I wasn't alone in the coach.

I heard and smelled nothing that wasn't built in to the en-
closure, which didn't signify anything. Anyone capable of
boarding a train in motion, and of surprising the conductor—
if that was the case—would have been clever enough to dis-
semble any outward evidence of his presence. Although young,
the conductor seemed to be no stranger to a coupling-pin and
its potential as weapon. If I wasn't tracking a ghost of my own
imagination, I was up against a serious reckoning.

At length I crept forward, leading the way with the revolver
and steadying myself against the sway of the car with my free
hand on the seats; swiveling my head left and right to deter-
mine that the swing-up footrests were the only things waiting
on the floor. I didn't neglect the brass-railed luggage racks overhead, looking for shadows that wouldn't stay still. My pulse
thumped in my ears. I could hear the sweat crackling down my
back.

Whoot-whoo-whoot! The locomotive's whistle exploded
hoarsely, sending my spine straight up through the crown of
my head. My fingers dug holes through velvet and horsehair,
the handle of the Deane-Adams creaked in my fist. I swallowed my heart and moved on.

Finishing a search with nothing to show for it is almost as
exhausting as hand-to-hand combat. It took as much out of a
man as swinging a bat with all his might and connecting with
nothing but air. At the front end of the car I leaned against
the wall for a moment, waiting for my breath to catch up and
the pounding in my chest to slow. I was getting too old for
most things, and most especially this. I tore loose my bandanna, mopped my face, used the last dry patch to wipe my

palms, changing hands in between, and put myself back together for the most challenging part of the operation.

Just to exhaust all the options, I went out onto the vestibule, climbed three rungs up the ladder bolted to the front of the coach, and checked the roofs of all four cars, then hung by one hand and swiveled to take in the tender and what I could see of the cab in front. I was a man holding a revolver with no target in sight. I stepped back down.

Of course, he might have ducked back down inside one of the cars I'd already searched. It was a shell game with an infinite number of shells, and all of them in control of the man running the game.

Fleetingly, I again considered pulling the cord to alert the engineer to stop the train; but if there was a stowaway riding in, say, the tender, that would be the signal to bail out and try his luck again down the line. I'd outgrown whatever patience I'd had to postpone the inevitable: Cut off the head of the octopus now rather than deal with its tentacles later.

Then I looked again at the tender.

Staring at the blank black pebbled surface of the cast-iron rear panel of the car, the wind lifting my hair and snatching at my coattails, I remembered the last time I'd clambered over one. It was as good a barrier as anything made by man against someone wanting to board the engine while a train is in motion. There were no catwalks, and the only handholds were the steel ladders welded at the corners for the wood-gatherers to deposit fuel in the black recess. Years had passed since I'd tried it the last time; my joints were more flexible then. Even so, it was blind luck alone that had kept me from falling and being dragged for a mile along the cinderbed.

I stepped back into the coach and jerked the cord.

THIRTEEN

Waiting for the engineer to come back and investigate the reason for the unscheduled stop, I returned to the vestibule, gun in hand, looking for anyone attempting to bail out of the tender. There was always the possibility that a stowaway had made his way to the locomotive, gotten the drop on the engineer and fireman, and having secured them was on his way to deal me out of the hand the same way he had the conductor; for by then I was convinced the young man was attracting ants somewhere in the wilderness between that lonely spot and where someone had bled on the floor of the caboose.

At length, a man wrapped in hard fat, filthy overalls, a smeared red bandanna around his neck, and a cap made of ticking came alongside the ties, swaying a little on solid ground with an eight-gauge shotgun clapped against one hip. To avoid any misunderstanding I holstered the Deane-Adams and leaned sideways across the iron railing, hands level with my shoulders. A pair of cut-back muzzles pointed at the underside of my chin, looking like paired artillery on the prow of a battlewagon.

"I been stuck up before," he said in the bawling voice of a man who'd broken his windpipe shouting over charging pistons. "Once by a man with a badge, just like you. I'm still here. Where they are depends on what they said to their Maker on the way over."

I asked him when was the last time he saw the conductor.

"You mean besides now, when he's standing behind you with a pistol aimed at your kidneys?"

I had to grin. It took sand to slide one from the bottom of the deck when you're being watched closely. "That one had rheumatism the first time I heard it. I asked because I don't think he's aboard."

"That ain't possible."

"Don't tell me you never lost a crew member. You didn't get that walk this week."

"What walk?" The shotgun drooped a little, but my trunk was still in his field of fire. "I lost a brakeman, two porters, and a fireman; dumb Hunky drank a pint of coal oil when he ran out of whiskey. I never lost no conductor and neither did any other engineer on the high line."

"That makes you a pioneer. He or somebody left some of his blood in the caboose."

"Probably barked his shin on the stove. Probably the young fool's wearing his first pair of long pants." He let the twin barrels dangle and planted a foot on the bottom step of the vestibule.

"If you're bent on covering the same ground I did, start with the caboose. I'll break the news to the lady inside."

He lifted the corner of his bandanna to mop his bulging brow. His fist-shaped jaw worked at something, but there was no bulge in his cheek to suggest he was chewing anything more than the wall of his mouth. Finally his foot thudded back down and he started toward the rear of the train, the scatter-gun level with his hip.

Mrs. Blackthorne was back in the day coach. She looked up from her basket of yarn. "Did we hit something?"

I told her what had happened. At first I left out the patch of blood; but she'd shared a parlor with her husband for thirty years while he brooded over the men he'd tried, which to release, which to imprison, which to stretch their necks. She was no garden lily. She seemed preoccupied with her knits and purls, but then so had Blackthorne with his gold-rimmed spectacles and pages of notes while officers of the court argued for and against the men and women in the dock; he'd often interrupt the recorder when he was asked to read from the transcript, finishing the testimony in question from memory.

"Could he have fallen off? Should we go back and look?" Her hands kept twirling at pace.

"If he had help falling off, that could be just what whoever gave him a hand wants us to do. We might back square into a mounted ambush."

"If that was the intent, why go to such lengths? They could have attacked us at any stop we made."

"It's an express. We stop only in settled cities, patrolled by officers. Anything can happen in this rough country, and no one can prove it happened at all."

"But to what purpose? Harlan gathered death threats the way some men amass stamps and silver, but the Almighty has beaten them all to the finish. Surely not I—"

"Your pardon, ma'am, but men with a debt to collect don't always write it off without looking back. When you've missed your chance at a buck . . ." I let it drop. I'd faced grizzlies and savages of all stripes, but a mannered woman in weeds is another challenge altogether.

". . . you bring down a doe. I think I understand you. A hot knife must temper itself in blood, any blood." She shook her head, her hands at rest at last. "This place will never know civilization. All the schools, churches, and halls of justice a man can build cannot turn wild dogs into lap hounds. What was it all about, all those years? Did you spill your spirit on barren sand?"

I had no answer for that, nor needed one. She wasn't addressing me.

A train at rest is a living thing, made though it is of planed wood and smelted iron; it throbs in place and shudders with every movement aboard. I felt the slight shift of a man's weight on the platform outside the rear door. The Deane-Adams was in my hand without my being aware that I'd gripped the handle. The engineer entered, cradling his shotgun. When he saw I was alone with the widow, he fisted his cap and swept it off his head.

"He's gone, sure enough. I seen—well, it ain't dry yet."

"I am aware the man bled," said Mrs. Blackthorne. "What do you propose to do?"

"We make a wood stop in Minnesota tonight. Company maintains a Western Union office, I suppose in case some squarehead logger chops his foot off. I'll wire the railroad in Minneapolis from there. Track gang's putting in a spur back in Bismarck. They can put together a search party. If he's off on a drunk he'll be digging coal come Decoration Day. Meanwhile we got a schedule to keep." He unshipped a turnip watch and snapped open the face, as if he needed confirmation we'd fallen behind.

"Anything could happen to the man before night," she said.

"Beg pardon, ma'am, but if it ain't happened by now it's already too late. Meanwhile the Northern Pacific's bigger than any one man." He swapped his watch for his cap, tugged it on, touched the bill, and swayed off through the door on the engine end.

"Company men." The needles resumed their blurring movement. "He left Washington to escape them and found one waiting at every stop."

More than one; but I took my own leave before pointing it out.

Back in the seat I'd selected I watched the scenery reverse itself momentarily while the train rocked back before resuming its eastward movement. The country resembled northern Oregon, where in 1889 I'd tracked a gang of bandits who'd been giving the stage line there one last dose of blue hell before the railroads shut it down. There an officious bastard with Wells and Fargo told me the company chief of detectives had the situation in hand, and why didn't I leg it back to wild country and see to the riffraff that was the specialty of the federal court. By then I'd committed Holy Scripture to memory and had chosen for my escutcheon "Go thou from the presence of a foolish man when thou perceivest not in him the fruits of wisdom." I wished him good luck and returned to the trail that had led me to Portland.

I found the head riffraff soaking the poisons out of his system in the Forbidden City Bath House across from the local railroad hotel, bubbles in his beard and a stump of cigar singeing the stubble. It was an accident, not that I bothered to inform the Judge of the circumstances when I gave him my report; I was wearing only a towel around my middle, and although I'd taken the precaution to tuck a belly gun behind my back, the man's own Smith Russian was closer to hand, hanging in its scabbard from the back of a wicked-looking chair carved into dragons and demons with a bottle of Black Tar finishing the process of ferment on the seat. He was starting to stir when I swept it up and laid the barrel across his near temple. Being a newly rediscovered Christian, I grabbed him by his hair as he slid into the water and saved him from drowning in a steaming tub stained with the blood of his scalp.

Not that he took it as an act of charity. When he came around, dressed (more or less) in the filthy rags he'd worn into the establishment, he swung a fist the size of a slab of bacon at my chin as I was fastening the last button on my shirt. I ducked it—I had all afternoon to do it, as some poisons remained in his system, slowing him like a freight wagon laboring up a steep grade—and finished the job with an elbow.

That was the easy part. Two blocks of muddy street separated us from the depot, where the 11:40 to Helena wasn't due for a quarter of an hour, and he wasn't likely to have billeted without the rest of his party somewhere about. I was dragging him down the boardwalk by his belt, his slack upper body bumping against my knee like scrap iron in a gunnysack, when a hornet buzzed past my jaw and slapped into clapboard belonging to a place that advertised itself as the only bowling alley between Salem and the Dominion of Canada. Not certain as to the angle, I drew, snapped a shot in the general direction of California, and slung my burden through the nearest unobstructed doorway, which happened to belong to a First Baptist Church: "Where the path to salvation is open to all."

Inside, wrapped in the odor of oiled wood, candle wax, and moth powder, a man who was as round as he was tall, with only a clerical collar separating the twin balloons of his torso and head, asked if my friend was in need of assistance. He had something between two slabs of coarse bread in one hand and a smear of mustard on his chin.

In earlier days I'd have let my revolver do my palavering, but I summoned enough of my newfound faith to put my business in the form of a request. "Sanctuary, Reverend. My friend and I require protection from the designs of wicked men."

I'll never know if my choice of words was sound. Just then another slug found its way through the door and took out a triangle of stained glass behind his left shoulder. The servant of Jesus threw his half-eaten sandwich toward where the shot had come from, swung about, and fled in the other direction through a door behind the pulpit.

I didn't judge him; it was the self-preservational version of turning the other cheek. Instead I found the edge of the door with my heel, swung it shut, and hauled my prize up the aisle the minister had gone (pausing briefly to ensure cooperation with a light tap from the handle of my revolver). Halfway to the pulpit I slung the baggage between pews and let it fall in a heap. I knelt beside it, leveling the barrel across the back of the pew.

Experience had taught me better. Bushwhackers never choose the front entrance. A barrage of lead erased most of the Annunciation from a window to the right, hurling daggers of glass across the room and slashing the back of the fine canvas coat I'd bought in Oregon City when the weather turned. I emptied two chambers in that direction, ducking just as another fusillade obliterated a pastoral scene in the window to my left. I was in the crossfire.

Any man who'd served Blackthorne as long as I had knew what to do in those circumstances. The bandit chief was slowing me down, and unlike the situation in *Frank Leslie's Illustrated Newspaper*, his life was no safe conduct when it came to men fighting for their own liberty; his followers would have put a bullet through him to get to me.

I shot him through both temples and was running for the door at the back before he hit the floor.

A shard of yellow wood leapt from the back of a pew as I passed. I spun to return fire and struck the broken pew with my elbow. Pain shot up my arm. The revolver jumped out of my hand and fell into the narrow aisle between the end of the row and the wall. Bandits can be prescient. They opened up a volley, aiming low and splintering wooden bun feet and floor planks. I gave up on retrieving my weapon and went into a sliding dive for the back door.

It led to a rectory, if that's not too lofty for simple Baptists: small, with presses containing volumes of a pious nature, a leather-topped desk supporting more books, scribbled foolscap, and a scatter of pennies—probably collected during services and awaiting entry in a ledger spread out on a drawleaf—a swivel, a tired armchair, and the good reverend in a water closet the size of a priest's hole, muttering what I took to be prayers. In the fetal position there was too much of him to close the door.

I wanted to join him; there was no exit except back into the church proper. A plain window had a splintered frame and a pile of broken glass at its base. A fresh bullet passed through the jagged opening and decapitated the glass chimney of an oil lamp on the desk, sending me to the floor. The gang had me penned in. I had minutes before one or more of them got up the sand to rush the building.

Just then a hoarse whistle entered the room, bent by distance; not enough to make up for the fact that probably for the first time all year the ll:40 was early. Unless there was a crowd of passengers waiting to board, the crew wouldn't wait, wanting as all railroaders do to get ahead of any unexpected delays down the line. The next train wasn't due for six more hours. Which unless I made this one was more than the sum total of my remaining lifespan.

"Is there a gun in the room?" I had to repeat the question at the top of my lungs.

"This is God's house," said the minister; but his one visible eye rolled upward.

A musket hung on a stone chimney above a fireplace at the back of the room. It had probably been used last to supply the church founders with game when it was under construction. Before that it might have come over on the original Oregon Trail forty years ago. But a gun is a gun.

I crawled and crabwalked to the fireplace, stood long enough to take the musket down off its pegs, and went back into a crouch when a new barrage destroyed the rest of the window frame. The musket was a wheel lock, and the iron pyrites some pioneer had last used to produce the spark was in place, likely rusted to the action. That was a break, if the mechanism wasn't a solid lump of rust. But if it blew up in my face it wouldn't change the odds against me.

The mule-ear-shaped hammer worked, at least, with a grating complaint. I worked it forward and back with both thumbs a couple of times to break loose some of the granules and seated it carefully. Using my knife I spent three times as long as I should have prying open a half-dozen shells from my cartridge belt and dumping the powder down the rust-caked muzzle; I dropped them often and had to scoop them up before they rolled out of my reach. I dumped the slugs down after the powder, but I wasn't satisfied.

Pennies.

I crawled and crabbed my way back to the desk, felt for the coppers, and threw a fistful down the barrel. Next I tore a piece off my shirttail for wadding and tamped it down with a length of shattered window frame. It was barely long enough with my thumb pushing it down the rest of the way. Another couple of minutes crawled past while I teased it back out with a little finger.

The rest was up to the bandits. If they proceeded in standard fashion, they'd leave a skeleton force to watch the windows and launch a full attack through the front door. But since when did outlaws keep to the standard?

I was as contented as I'd ever been. I hadn't a thing to lose, and that is a liberating feeling.

On hands and knees I returned to the room where services were conducted, went sideways, and stood with my back to the wall behind the pulpit. Again I tugged back the hammer, not far enough to lock it, keeping it from snapping forward with the tension of my thumb; expecting the trigger to be in working order was testing faith beyond acceptable limits.

Now I had a clear view of the street door just as it opened and four men came through. One had a lever-action repeater with its butt braced against his hip; the others held out long-barreled revolvers at arm's length, shoulder high, all aimed my direction. I couldn't describe any of the men, not after all these years or at that moment, but I could report the make and model of each weapon.

One of them smiled, at least; I saw that much. The sight of that ancient weapon was the funniest thing he'd seen that day.

And ever would. I let go of the hammer and opened my path to salvation.

FOURTEEN

——

Was it absolutely necessary to kill your prisoner? Could you not merely have rendered him insensible a few minutes longer?"

"I had a train to catch."

"One more impertinence and I'll find you in contempt. My court is wherever I am."

We were in the Judge's kitchen. Regardless of his caseload—which at its lightest would break Jumbo's back—he never entered the courthouse on the Sabbath. Mrs. Blackthorne was conducting a meeting of the Lewis and Clark County Ladies Civic Improvement League in the parlor, and with the chef away on his day off we had the room to ourselves. It was large and square, with a low discolored ceiling, a massive six-lid stove, an ice box to match, and a long cedar table scoured as white as scraped bone. The floor was solid stone and the lath-

and-plaster walls, once painted green, had taken on a saffron color, a visual memory of thousands of meals prepared there, along with the ghosts of grease, onion, sauerbraten, and brook trout turning the air as thick as lard. Blackthorne, in his waistcoat with his cuffs turned back past his thick forearms, was slicing a salami the size of his thigh with a knife sinisterlooking enough to have been borrowed from the attic evidence room above his chambers. (It might have, at that; he disliked straining the court's budget with personal expenses.)

"I wasn't being impertinent, Your Honor." *Not entirely.* "The odds against my clearing town in a position useful to the court couldn't be bigger unless he came around while I was facing his cohorts." There was some diplomacy in my choice of vocabulary; *cohorts* was one of his favorite terms for the men and women he'd been appointed to prosecute; he preferred—or pretended—to consider himself a nineteenth-century bulwark between the citizens in his jurisdiction and the legions of wicked old Rome. Substituting *useful to the court* for *leaving Portland alive* was similar strategy. A deputy never went wrong reminding the old man of his service to the judiciary.

He used the knife to spear the slice he'd cut, poked it into his mouth, and pushed the salami my way, impaling it with the knife. He chewed and swallowed before continuing; Washington manners prevailed even in Helena. "You killed two men, maimed a third for life, and I expect to hear any time of the demise of the fourth. The others evidently fled after the explosion." He poured slugs of brandy into two snifters, took a sip from one, and wobbled it around his mouth before committing it to his system. "Why pennies, incidentally? Dimes are the usual choice when shot is scarce."

"It's a poor congregation."

"Ah. It's a shame you didn't wander into a Presbyterian. As I was saying. I should bill you, if not for those burials, then for the man Corrigan, whom you slew in cold blood."

He appeared to weigh the matter, swirling the thistle-colored liquid in his glass and reading my future in its depths; but I'd seen his performance on the bench often enough to know that was theater. His serious decisions were always made in private. The die was cast before I'd entered the house. I helped myself to a nervous gulp from my glass regardless. Taking him for granted would earn me another hour on the carpet.

"However," he said; and I felt the warmth of the word crawling up my spine along with the spirits. "He was sought dead or alive for the murder of a shotgun messenger, so at all events his life was forfeit. Apart from the collateral damage in the press about defiling the sanctity of the church, I cannot find serious fault with your decision, although if I found myself in those circumstances I should have considered an alternative. The journals and I are old adversaries; this court is no worse off for the affair."

I nodded, biting into the slice of salami I'd cut for myself. It was an appropriate enough response on my part that meant nothing. I didn't tell him I hadn't been aware of Corrigan's dead-or-alive status until that moment.

A lurch woke me in the day coach; I'd grown accustomed to the sensation of the train coming to a stop. I was back in the world post-Blackthorne. My window was dark. I thought we'd stopped in a tunnel, but night had fallen. I hadn't slept that long or that deeply during the day in years. I felt a sting of panic, of having let down my guard in a tense situation. That, too, was recent. Had all my stores of instinct based on experience played out just because my service was coming to an end?

In my lap, one hand still held my Bible open to Lamentations ("The yoke of my transgressions is bound by His hand: They are wreathed, and come up upon my neck; He hath made my strength to fall, the Lord hath delivered me into their hands, from whom I am not able to rise up"), the other the Deane-Adams, which I'd left in its holster when I sat down. My reflexes, at least, were still in force.

I looked around. The lanterns were lit, probably by Caspar, the only member of the paid crew whose duties didn't nail him to his station. The engineer must have taken him into the fold. I could feel the locomotive breathing in and out, as if I were straddling the back of a beast at rest. There was no sign of Mrs. Blackthorne. I put away the Bible and got up, holding the revolver snug to my hip.

A window near the front of the car gave me a better view of our surroundings. Steam from the jets drifted in front of flames crawling in a stone pit, the light limning a block-shaped building and figures carrying something heavy on their shoulders in the direction of the train. A sweetish smell of fresh-cut pine told me we were in the wood camp just across the border. Another obstruction stood on a railroad siding, coughing thick balls of smoke toward the stars, obscuring them at ragged intervals; this was no pale woodsmoke, but the tarry exhaust of hard coal. When the wind shifted, redirecting the flames, I got a glimpse of what it was. I straightened and went looking for the widow.

We nearly collided in the sleeper. She wore a thick flannel robe over a nightgown whose plain gray hem came to the insteps of old suede slippers, worn to the shapes of her toes. She and I retired and arose on separate schedules, so it was the first time I'd seen her with her hair down, wound into a plait and draped forward over her left shoulder. Silver strands glistened among the white in the muted light of one of the two lamps that illuminated the car fore and aft. Even so, she looked younger with the pins out. A phantom of the comely girl she'd been glimmered behind the creases in her face. I had enough of my own, without the beauty.

"We have stopped," she said.

"For fuel. We're in Minnesota."

"What time is it?"

"I didn't look. Not late, I don't think."

"That means we will be in St. Paul before tomorrow evening. We must see Morton, the lawyer, first thing the next morning."

"A lot can happen between now and then," I said. "Hearst's *Javelin* is here."

Her face assumed an expression I'd seen on the Judge's face when a counselor tried to bat something past him. "Will that pestilence never abate?" She nearly spat the words.

"Just now they may have more to tell us than we them."

"I cannot imagine what that could be."

"Are you sure? Everywhere we've been, they're either already there waiting for us or minutes behind. I want to ask Howard Rossleigh which they were when our conductor disappeared."

FIFTEEN

I took a stroll through the camp. The laborers helping the fireman load the tender paid less attention to me than to the gnats dancing woozily around the chunks of wood on their shoulders. They smelled of honest sweat, sweet chaw, frying onions, and smoke from the fire pit they used for cooking. Those odors mingled with the scents of fresh-cut pine, cedar, and sycamore; the men breathed them in like fish filtering oxygen from water. To them, the swift little yard engine dozing on the siding was all of a piece with the hognose locomotives that bore logs from the sawmill to flatboats and from them to the world beyond. Very little came between men who sawed and chopped and portaged the materials that built a nation and their day's work.

Not that *The Javelin* was designed to blend into any wilderness. Inspired apparently by the gaudy White Train that carried Buffalo Bill's Wild West between coasts, the publisher had enameled it from caboose to cowcatcher till it shone like alabaster. A brace of flags flapped fore and aft: to the right Old Glory, to the left the spread-eagle masthead of *The New York Morning Journal* embroidered in blue and white on a field of red. Forward-leaning italics bore the train's name in a continuous frieze along the sides of the cars, with a javelin underscoring it in case the meaning was lost on the casual observer. Everything about this whorehouse on wheels glistened, even the costly blue coal heaped in the tender.

I sauntered around the boiler. Block letters painted in a semicircle on the front of the boiler read W. R. HEARST, PROP.

I'd seen his kind before, nursing their gout in Scottish castles set on a thousand acres of prairie in Wyoming, smoking six-bit cigars in gentlemen's clubs in Denver and St. Louis, soaking in porcelain tubs in private railroad cars on the Oregon high line, flashing gold teeth dug from their own mines in San Francisco; fat jaspers who'd either inherited their wealth or piled it up so quickly and so long ago they couldn't distinguish between a cartwheel dollar and a trunk filled with double eagles. This one had stepped from the cradle into a ton of silver, built on the back of a forty-dollar mule long since repossessed for payment of a delinquent debt owed by his father. Since then, the son had trebled the family fortune, opening newspapers in most of the major cities across the U.S., then cut it in half buying putative medieval furniture, ancient Spanish chapels to be disassembled and shipped across the Atlantic, and exotic animals he let roam free on his many estates. When his private parlor car kept waking him up during train-changes, he bought a train. He would pay a hundred thousand dollars for an armoire reputed to have stood in the king's bedroom at Versailles (but made in Grand Rapids,

Michigan, with wormholes bored with a brace-and-bit manufactured in Detroit), but he couldn't quote you the price on
a piece of penny candy.

There's no arguing it: All the people who know how to be
rich aren't.

A basset-faced engineer sat with his elbow on the ledge of
the cab opening, leaning out to read a folded newspaper in the
light of the lamp mounted on the side of the engine, moving
his lips over the columns of gray print. I walked past without
stirring him, climbed the steps to the vestibule of the only passenger car, and knocked on the door. I couldn't remember if
I'd ever done that aboard a train. A low-register female voice
called an invitation from inside.

It was a private coach a step or two down from the top of
the Pullman line, paneled in blond ash with machine-woven
carpeting, a walnut secretary with a leaf that dropped down
like the trapdoor in the seat of flannel underdrawers, a berth
folded up against the curved ceiling, and a pair of club chairs
upholstered in green plush. The woman seated in front of the
secretary wore a pale blue linen shirtwaist starched stiff as
clapboard siding, an ankle-length gray wool skirt hitched up
on one side to prevent tripping over the hem when the train
was in motion, and a flat-brimmed straw hat pinned to a pile
of upswept hair that caught the lamplight in haloes of red. Her
nails were trimmed short of the current fashion, probably to
expedite the blurring motion of her fingers over the pearl-
inlaid keys of a black iron typewriter on the dropleaf. The
strikers hit the sheet rolled onto the platen with a noise like
pebbles hitting a snare drum.

She went on typing without looking up until a bell rang and
she masher-slapped the carriage back into place. A pair of

hazel eyes under green-tinted lids found mine through pinch-nose spectacles. She unclamped them and rubbed at the little dents they'd made on her bridge.

I showed her my star. "I'm looking for Harold Rossleigh."

"Me, too, along with every stringer between here and New York." Those low-hanging tones reminded me of someone, though I couldn't place her just then. The West seemed to be filling up with women who commanded attention without raising their voice. "You're Page Murdock."

It wasn't a question, so I didn't answer it. "You've lost your boss reporter?"

"*I'm* the boss reporter. Betsy Pike." She got up and came over with her hand out, perpendicular to the elbow, the way a man offered his. As she rose, her skirt came down, cheating me of a closer look at a smoothly muscled limb shrouded in sheer black.

Since it was right there in front of me I took the hand. She had the grip of an athletic boy. The tips of her fingers were cal-lused.

"What name do you use when you cash a bank draught?" I said.

She flushed slightly—I thought; her coloring was naturally high. "Pamela Green. The byline was the Chief's idea. Mr. Hearst?" She went on as if I'd reacted to the magic name. "He never choked down having to send a reporter to interview Nellie Bly—right name Elizabeth Cochrane—when she fin-ished her round-the-globe trip for *The New York World* in fewer than eighty days. The *Journal* and Mr. Pulitzer's *World* have been at war since Hector was a pup."

"I'm a poor substitute for the Grand Tour."

"The Chief carries his apery only so far. He might steal a competitor's idea, or even his staff, but he won't trail him across old ground. Meanwhile *The Javelin* was wasting itself switching cars in a railyard in Sacramento. It was like hitching Pegasus to a milk wagon."

"What did you mean about everyone looking for Rossleigh?"

"Just that. He got off in Bismarck to join the reporters aboard your train during the stop and never came back. Our esteemed colleagues didn't see which way he went after they separated to file their stories. I had to convince the Chief they actually saw him leave your train; he was all fired up to force Grover Cleveland to order your arrest by the Secret Service."

"I've been arrested before. I understand they eat well in Leavenworth. How much do you know about Rossleigh?"

She breathed on her spectacles and wiped the lenses on her sleeve. They'd sparkled even before that. "Don't let my gender cloud your reason. I'm a reporter. It's my job to ask questions, not answer them."

"Mine, too; before this damn trip."

"Let's trade. What difference does knowing Rossleigh's character make to you?"

Age had mellowed me. In earlier days I'd have gotten what I wanted by force. Gender had never clouded my reason; not in that area. "Who's asking, you or your rag?"

"I'll warn you before we go on the record."

"I guess I'll have to accept that. If you agree to tell me everything you know about Howard Rossleigh."

"Agreed. I should tell you it isn't much."

"That makes us even. All I know is our conductor went missing somewhere between here and Bismarck, leaving behind a jigger of blood."

"His or someone else's?"

It was important to put aside the frills and frippery and remember she was a reporter. "A prairie hen, for all I know."

"And you suspect my partner just because he vanished around the same time?"

"I suspect your whole damn train. It's been on ours like whitewash since we left Helena. Start with how a man who works for the Montana Press Association came to represent a chain of newspapers based in New York City."

"Seven years ago, when the territory became a state, he wrote a series of articles about the importance of the process. The wire services picked it up and spread it across the country. It was Independence Day week, so all the major papers jumped all over it in the name of patriotism. The Chief was impressed enough to take him on as a stringer. Personally, I found his writing full of stale platitudes, split infinitives, and dangling participles; but the man I work for couldn't distinguish between a first predicate and the Tenth Commandment."

Neither could I, nor just what a platitude or infinitive or participle was; but to interrupt her would be ungentlemanly.

"Harlan Blackthorne's death," she went on, "put Rossleigh in the saddle of the story of the year. He intends to ride it all the way to a position as managing editor of the *Journal*. He might, at that. The bold stroke is the coin of Mr. Hearst's realm."

"But not yours."

"I don't have a realm, or the scepter necessary to rule it." Spinning her spectacles by the end of their ribbon, she searched my face for comprehension of just what she'd said. She got nothing; I'd served the court across as many poker tables as I had across the Great Plains.

The eyeglasses swung to a smacking stop in her other palm. "In the perfect world, I'd be conducting interviews aboard Blackthorne's funeral train instead of correcting Rossleigh's grammar and syntax. However, the world isn't perfect, even on the frontier, where a colored man is judged by the quality of his work, while a woman is but a woman, white or otherwise."

She returned to the desk and sat, her skirt and petticoats rustling like wind stirring a field of corn, and placed the spectacles astraddle her nose. "So you see, Marshal, Howard Rossleigh has no interest in depriving your party of a conductor. I'm not suggesting he isn't capable of the worst of crimes; only that in this case there's no percentage in it for him."

"Why do you sound like you're disappointed?"

My gaze must have slipped to her exposed stocking. She swiveled, inserting it in the kneehole, and snatched off her glasses. Exposed, her eyes pinned me to the wall. "I can handle mashers. It isn't that."

"I suppose a hat like that needs a long and wicked pin to hold it in place."

Her smile was bitter. "I'm not a dried-up spinster taking a shortcut through the Central Park." She slid open the belly drawer and took out a Marston derringer no more than five inches long from butt to front sight. It was plated in a mirror finish and the grips were pearl.

"It's cute. Does it fire bullets or beans?"

"The Chief thinks I'm petite. He gave it to me when the police broke a triple murder in Brooklyn Heights and I beat the *World* to the story. I'd have preferred an Army Colt; but you don't look a gift gun in the muzzle."

"The drawer's okay, but you should lock it if you really want to slow down your draw."

She returned it and slid shut the drawer. "I recognized you. Mr. Hearst hired his house artist out from under the chief of

police. He could draw the *Mona Lisa* from a cabled description without ever having seen it. Your reputation doesn't include harming law-abiding women."

I shook my head. A reporter of all people should know you
can't believe everything you read.

SIXTEEN

____

She deposited the spectacles on the dropleaf desk beside the typewriter, planted an elbow on the other side, and rested her chin in her cupped palm, looking at me. I'd begun to form a theory about those eyeglasses, but the time hadn't come to test it just yet. Her eyes took on a hard metallic sheen when she applied them to a close study.

"Is it true you faced down the entire Mercy Gang?"

I grinned.

"'The Mercy Gang,' is that what they're calling it now? When I first met them they were the Mercy brothers, scourge of highwaymen, bushwhackers, and men of low character in general. Reputation is a seasonal thing."

"You didn't answer the question. Did you wipe them out or didn't you?"

"You can ask Jordan Mercy himself when he gets back from Europe with Buffalo Bill's outfit."

"You're an impossible interview."

"I'm not an interview of any kind. When do you expect to hear back from your people about what became of Rossleigh?"

"Also relentless. Is it something you learned from Black-thorne, or did you bring it with you? What did you do before that, incidentally? The record's spotty regarding your early life."

"According to Jack Rimfire I stopped Pickett's Charge with no assistance from the federal army."

"I don't count what the nickel novelists say. They make up all sorts of outrageous things to fill in the blanks."

I couldn't hold out any longer. I snatched up her spectacles and peered through them. The lenses were plain glass. I put them back. "As I thought. You need a stage property so people will take you for a serious journalist instead of an uncommonly pretty woman."

"Not so uncommon in New York; although P. T. Barnum offered me a job to stand in for Jenny Lind."

"You turned him down?"

"I chose not to offend him with a refusal. He made the decision himself after he heard me sing."

"I'm not the yokel you think. She died when you were in grammar school. I thought you reporters set store in the truth."

"In print, yes. Is your past so black you won't share it even now?"

"Is Rossleigh's so black you won't tell me what he's about?"

"I've changed my mind. You're not relentless, merely a bore." She pushed herself back, opened a cabinet in the bottom of the secretary, and hoisted a rosewood case onto her lap by its rolled leather handle. It was cathedral-shaped, with a pair of doors in front secured with a brass latch. She worked the latch and swung them wide, exposing a crystal decanter held in place with a leather strap and a quartette of cut-glass footed goblets in plush-lined cylinders. "I had to smuggle this aboard. The Chief's teetotal and expects the same from his staff. I needn't tell you the deep drawer of every desk in the office is locked. It's the wettest place in town outside of Delmonico's cellar." She unstopped the decanter. "I won't insult you by offering you a pull from the bottle of Old Liver-Eater that Howard squirreled away in the caboose. You're a drinking man, of course."

"A question phrased as a sentence is still a question." I scooped out a pair of goblets and set them on the leaf.

"Napoleon brandy," she said, filling them a third of the way with liquid the color of thistle honey. "A misnomer, to improve sales. The Little Corporal drank wine only."

"A historian as well as a scribbler." I drew up one of the armchairs, sat, and touched my glass to hers. They rang like silver bells. "To Howard's safe return from the wilderness."

"To his return, anyway. If he's not back on the reservation come next week, I'll be on my way East in a public chair car." She sipped. "This assignment is my ticket-of-leave from the Stunt Feature Bowery. I didn't accept it to spend the rest of my career riding circus elephants and interviewing lady mountain climbers." She hesitated, then put down the rest in one jerk. This time her face flushed to the roots of her hair. Even then she might have carried it off, but a harsh little cough brought a wad of lace handkerchief to her lips.

I chose not to pour coal oil on that fire with a remark, however appropriate. I barely wet my whistle, the way the Judge had instructed me in the gentlemanly arts. The stuff was as good as his brandy, but lacked the mellow smoke of his Scotch whiskey. I replenished her glass without asking. Just the introduction of spirits into the conversation seemed to have pried loose her tongue.

"I'd be open to considering his disappearance a coincidence if our conductor hadn't taken a sabbatical at the same time," I said. "The only thing that keeps me from clamping those slender wrists in iron is *why*."

She turned one, examining it as if it belonged to someone else. "Are they slender? I grew up milking cows on a farm in Ohio. Papa said I could arm-wrestle Sandor the Magnificent."

"You couldn't find Ohio if you boarded an express train."

Her face betrayed nothing of her failure. She'd tried to exchange a lead slug for a coin of truth about my own background and we'd both heard the thud.

"I crossed the northeast corner on the way from Philadelphia to Detroit to cover the unveiling of the world's largest cook stove. The Michigan Stove Company engaged a family to live in it for a month. The Chief sold the company two pages of advertising at a thousand dollars a pop and I got two days off to visit my cousin in Buffalo. One of them was Washington's birthday."

I said, "I'm a poor investment. I haven't anything to advertise."

"When it comes to boosting circulation, Page Murdock's life story is almost as good as a war in Cuba. A dash of scarlet on those gray columns is like raw meat to a pack of dogs."

"I'm retired. I'm trading my guns for a chair by the fire."

She shook her head. "You're still good copy. You don't know Mr. Hearst. Once he gets his teeth in a thing he never lets go."

"Then he'll replace you if Rossleigh doesn't turn up."

She smiled. "I'm sure he'll be thinking that; but I've a pretty good set of choppers of my own."

We were at a deadlock: Force checked, object unmoved. A whistle blew; the funeral train was fueled up and ready to pull out. I put away the rest of my drink and rose. We promised to share developments. I think for a moment we actually believed we would. Her infernal machine resumed clacking as I stepped to the ground.

As we slowed for a crossing, the climbing sun broke through a dirty scrim of cloud and fell full on a white frame building with a steeple. Mrs. Blackthorne directed me to signal for a stop. I traded my old duck traveling coat for the Prince Albert I'd packed in my valise and we attended the Sunday service at the Grace Lutheran Church.

I was overdressed, as it turned out. The village was a farming community, and clean overalls under a rusty tailcoat was the male uniform. The women in print dresses cut glances at the widow, but the curiosity was directed more toward the lavender and lace she wore than who she was: The only newspaper, *The Weekly Democrat*, occupied a storefront down the street; its latest number had probably run before the Judge's death was announced, so the existence of the funeral train hadn't preceded it there.

The church was the only place of worship in that two-block arrangement of mercantile, barber shop, livery, blacksmith, and post office, but my companion was the tolerant sort: Apart from an occasional tightening of the lips, scorn for rituals foreign to Presbyterian didn't manifest itself. Several of the hymns were familiar to us both. She had a strong, clear voice, unclogged and unroughened by years of use. The minister, white-haired, horse-faced, and clean-shaven, delivered a brief sermon from St. Luke, regarding the Lord's forty-day sabbatical in the wilderness, which drew a quiet smile from Mrs. Blackthorne, and I suppose from myself, although I took care to conceal it, not knowing if the Judge had told her I'd shared her reference to the passage the day they'd arrived in Helena, or if she'd consider it a violation of the marital code.

When the ceremony was over we joined the queue greeting the minister at the door. When the lady laid her gloved hand in his palm, he remarked that hers was a new face in the congregation.

"Beatrice Blackthorne, Reverend. I enjoyed your sermon."

His expression didn't change, but his eyes went alight. "I thought perhaps it was you," he said. "That would make this gentleman Mr. Murdock?"

That came as a surprise, in view of the general apathy regarding the strangers in the community's midst. I said, "It would make me Mr. Murdock. I'm not sure about the gentleman part."

"A boy asked me to give you this message. He didn't know the man who gave it to him."

He drew a fold of paper from under his robe and put it in my hand.

"Go with God," he said.

"I always do," said the lady.

I waited until we were outside and the crowd was thinning before opening it. Mrs. Blackthorne clutched her wrap at her throat, watching me read.

It was scribbled in pencil, in a script barely legible:

> *I am in the livery. Come alone, and make sure no one sees you go inside.*
>
>   *H. Rossleigh*

SEVENTEEN

The widow studied the note I'd handed her.

"Are we certain Rossleigh wrote this?"

"The reverend said a boy delivered it, at the request of a stranger. I've never seen a sample of Rossleigh's handwriting, but I can't think what anyone would have to benefit from impersonating him."

"You should find the boy and ask for a description."

"No time. Our bird may get restless and fly the coop."

"He makes no mention of our missing conductor. He may be innocent after all; just another journalist in quest of a story."

We stood under a porch roof shared by several buildings, all of them closed on Sunday. With the merchants gone and most of the devoted Lutherans on their way home to prepare and eat luncheon, we had the business district to ourselves.

I said, "That's one side of the coin. The other is he wants to make me a stationary target."

"I suppose you must look at it that way. Of course you will not accept the invitation."

"Shall I be rude, then?"

She didn't honor that with a response. I felt a little ashamed for having said it. She'd earned better than my characteristic stance. I switched tracks.

"It's a chance we can't afford to pass up. Until now he's been asking all the questions. He owes us answers. We'll begin with how he managed to beat us to this wide spot in the road without *The Javelin* and work our way back from there."

"You persist in saying 'we,' but he said to come unaccompanied. You should not go there alone, however. There must be some kind of authority in this settlement."

"If they could afford a full-time marshal and not just a noon-breaker, they could afford a depot and a telegraph office. A dry-goods clerk with a cap-and-ball Colt he keeps in a sugar jar is as likely to shoot himself in the knee as a bushwhacker. Then again, it might be *my* knee he shoots. I'm better off having to look in only one direction."

"You do not place much faith in your fellow traveler, do you?"

"I started out with plenty. It doesn't grow back."

I escorted her back to the train, checked the load in the Deane-Adams again, and made my way to the livery, holding the revolver in the right saddle pocket of my frock coat. A man carrying open draws too much curiosity in a town that size. I should have changed back into the duck; I'd lost two good city coats having to fire through the pocket when there wasn't time to draw, but I don't like being late for appointments, especially when they're with someone who might be inclined not to give me time to clear my weapon.

Nothing about the building differed from every other barn

I'd visited: the same steep-pitched roof, the same boards pegged up vertically with gaps between you could sling a cat through, the same double doors reinforced with crossed planks, closed now but with the padlock hanging from a hasp torn loose of its screws. Being an experienced reporter, Rossleigh would show the usual disrespect to equipment designed to keep him at bay.

I grasped the rusted handle belonging to the left door, swung it wide, and let go of the handle to grip the top board with my free hand, riding it all the way around. That kept me from making a target inside the frame. I banged up against the outside wall and hung there, waiting for the fireworks. All that came out was a gust of sweet grain, manure, ammonia, and animal sweat; a not-unpleasant odor to anyone who'd spent his life around it, and not as bad as some. Whoever took care of the place kept on top of the important chores.

I hopped to the ground, then moving at sloth's pace I edged around the door, hand and revolver now in the open, and yanked it shut behind me with my boot heel hooked on the bottom crossboard. That put me in near-twilight, the late-morning sun parsed into narrow slits with clouds of fine chaff roiling in the current of air churned up by the door's sweep. At first glance nothing about the place stood apart from every other stable in my experience: A loft twelve feet above the earth floor heaped with straw, a stout ladder leading up to it, narrow stalls at the back, saddles lined up on a wooden rail, a barrel stove (unlit on a fair spring day), a split-bottom chair performing double duty as a hall tree with a shapeless canvas coat hanging from the back, a pair of manure-stained Wellington boots leaning drunkenly against each other, and the obligatory brass spittoon placed a sporting distance from whoever occupied the chair when the place was open for business.

A cone of wood shavings lay before the chair, with the whittling knife thrust up to its haft in the dirt. I'd never seen the point; but then I knew my letters for when it came to whiling away the empty hours.

Nothing happened beyond the ordinary. Even the horses in the stalls greeted the unscheduled visit with no more enthusiasm than snorts and a loud splatter of horse-apples. A couple of them went on munching the fodder in their nosebags, sounding like infantry boots marching through gravel; I meant less to them than a mouthful of soggy oats. But then I never had, not even when I was the one who supplied the oats. Ours was a relationship based on necessity, like baggy dungarees and a pair of suspenders. I'd never ridden a horse that had a name I gave it. The supply lines can get long, and it's not a good idea to get misty about what might be next week's blue-plate special.

I swept the place with my eyes, cocked my ears for creaks in the loft, let out the breath I'd been holding since I opened the door, and seated the hammer on the Deane-Adams.

Which was a mistake.

The tread of hundreds of feet and hooves had pounded the dirt floor as solid as bedrock; the slug slammed into it with a ringing noise like a tack-hammer striking iron, chucking bits of earth up over the toe of my right boot. The report came hard on its echo, a sharp snap that sounded hardly lethal in the openness of the space inside the barn.

I knew better. I landed on my right shoulder, sliding with the momentum, firing as I went, at an oblique upward angle, aping as close as possible the trajectory of the first bullet from pure instinct. The .45 made a deeper, rounder report, crack-ling into one of the floorboards in the loft; an axe makes just such a noise biting into a trunk. I sent two more after it, spread-ing my field of fire, while I was still sliding. I came to rest with a sudden sickening thud against one of the six-by-six beams that held up the building, striking it with my other shoulder; hard enough to remember it today in damp weather.

Another shot came from the loft. This time I saw the pow-der flare in a gap between boards. I put the money shot on that spot, but I knew as I sent it that it wouldn't hit anything mor-tal. There's a kind of melancholy strain in a parting report, one intended to give the party on the other end a moment to make his withdrawal.

> Defense: Your Honor, I object. The witness is indulging in fantasy. A shot is a shot; no gunman is capable of express-ing his emotions by way of a mechanical device.
> Blackthorne: The jury will disregard the witness's answer and the reporter will strike it from the record. The bench in-structs the witness to adhere to known facts.

What plays in the moment never works in court; but judge, counsel, and jury are always absent when the moment comes. I knew before I heard the scrape of a sole and the rustle of clothing that my shooter had taken his exit through the win-dow in the loft.

I sprang up before I heard the thump of feet striking the ground outside from a one-story leap, but running as fast as my legs would straighten, I missed the ambusher. I got to the back corner of the stable in a couple of seconds, just in time to see the dust settle where an alley intersected with the street that ran behind the building.

Reloading as I walked, I retraced my steps, found the dimple in the earth where the first bullet had buried itself, and poked around with the blade of my clasp knife. After a moment it touched something even harder than the packed dirt. I slid the point to the bottom and pried, teasing the object free like a splinter from my thumb. When the slug came to light I plucked it up between thumb and forefinger, rolled it into my palm, and flipped it a couple of times, coin fashion, guessing its weight. It confirmed what I'd expected from the sound of the report, and opened a new mystery regarding space and time.

The print of my boot where I'd stood was still visible in the grain dust that covered the floor. Two inches separated the toe from where the lump of lead had stopped. That was more than a near-miss: It was surgery.

EIGHTEEN

Y ou're gonna wear that bit o' lead down to a BB, doncha know."

I stopped turning the slug around in my fingers and looked at the man seated across from me in his bentwood rocker. He was a Swede, tall and thin but for his belly. He was basically a garden hose with a croquet ball stuck halfway down its length. His striped trousers would belong to his Sunday suit, the belt fastened above his paunch. His shirt was white, clean but threadbare at the elbows where pink showed through, and buttoned to the neck. Swags of skin hung down over where the collar would go if he wore one. His face was two sizes too large for his skull; if he had eyes in the slits that canted down from the bridge of his beak of a nose it would take a bull's-eye lantern to locate them. His hair was white, fine as sugar, and combed in three precise lanes across his long skull. His name was Lundergaard, and he was all that stood between the good citizens of town and the lawless abyss. I don't know if the community issued him a badge; in any case he wouldn't put holes in what was probably his one good shirt.

"It's a small round for the work it was put to." I examined it once more before slipping it into the side pocket of my coat. "I thought maybe you'd know someone who packs light."

He pulled at his lower lip, which didn't return to its earlier position when he let go. He was seventy, figuring charitably. "I don't believe I've seen a hip gun round here in years. The rifles and shotguns don't come out till hunting season, doncha know. Just at this moment I can't say for sure what I did with my Dragoon."

"Check the sugar jar."

We were in the parlor of his house. It was one of the original log cabins from lumber camp days, but someone with a yen for civilization had sided it with clapboard and smeared the interior walls with plaster and paper. Bulging gilt frames hung high on the walls, allowing some old wheezes with monkey whiskers and sharp-faced dragons in bombazine to scowl down at us from beyond the grave. You couldn't blow your nose without bumping into something on a pedestal. A parlor stove glowed through colored mica. You could can preserves in that room without a kettle, and on a fair spring day; Marshal and Mrs. Lundergaard hadn't broken a sweat since Buchanan. I shifted my weight on the fainting couch, hoping not to stain the peach-colored cushions.

"I had to guess, I'd say some young sprout found his papa's squirrel gun after morning services and took a poke at a crow. You and the livery just got in the way."

"That doesn't explain the note."

He hooked wires over his big ears and peered again at

Rossleigh's note through thick panes of glass, moving his lips over the words. "I still don't see this feller's beef, or why he'd take the trouble of tying himself to your killing by signing his name."

"There's no reason you should. That's as good a reason as any to find him, so we can ask."

"I'll look into it if you like." He returned the note. His jowls went on shaking after his mouth stopped, doing for his head what he was too polite to do himself.

I let him stew a few seconds. He'd be as useful in a manhunt as a screen door on a diving bell, but that was no reason not to stir up his dried-out perspiration glands.

"It isn't worth your valuable time, Marshal." I got up and held out my hand. "Thanks for seeing me."

He took it, in a grip I'd have thought he'd left behind at Appomattox. "Don't be in such a rush, son. You've not lived till you sampled Esther's cracklin's."

The house smelled of hot grease. I cleared my throat to cover the grumbling in my stomach. I hadn't eaten in fifteen hours. "Next time through," I said. "The Judge won't keep much longer."

I let myself out. I could feel his relief all the way to the door.

"He'd see that old fool was broken down to streetsweep," Mrs. Blackthorne said.

He would be the late departed; in her world there was only one masculine occupant. "I told you not to expect too much," I said. "We're the invaders here. As he sees it, we brought the trouble with us. Every community has some charged-up boy you can blame for any disturbance. No self-respecting part-time peace officer would find himself without one handy."

"Then you still suspect Rossleigh for what happened to our conductor."

"If it is Rossleigh, he didn't care one way or the other about the conductor except as a potential obstacle. He had to be sacrificed in order to clear the way to the target."

"But who is the target, you or me?"

"I'm hoping it's me. I make more sense, and I've taken care of myself in that situation enough times to count on experience. If—and pardon me for the suggestion—the situation were reversed, and it was you in that box in the caboose and the Judge sitting in this coach, my money would be on the Judge. When it comes to enemies, he was as rich as J. P. Morgan. I'm just well-to-do."

"He always said his mortal foes were beads in his Rosary. He never explained why he felt it necessary to invoke the Church of Rome."

"I'm still wondering how Rossleigh beat us to town. There's no sign of *The Javelin*."

Outside, a moose roared.

"What on earth was that?" she asked.

It came again, a long guttural, like a creature moaning in anguish.

I was sitting opposite the widow in one of a pair of facing seats. I got up, the Deane-Adams sliding into my hand on its own. "If this was Canada, I'd guess—"

Another noise came on the heels of the first, fully as deep but brassy. Then all hell joined in: The bow dragging across the strings of a cello, the measured flatulence of a tuba, the *ting* of a triangle, and the general conspiracy of trumpet, bass drum, cymbals, flute, and slide trombone:

After the ball is over;
after the break of morn,
After the dancers' leaving,
After the stars are gone . . .

"Oh, dear Lord." She closed her eyes.

I bent to look out the window. The members of the band hadn't taken the time to change out of their Sunday best; I could practically smell the moth powder drifting from the platform where they'd assembled to saw, blow, and beat at their instruments, splintering the notes sharply enough to pierce the Judge's coffin and roust him from his heavenly rest.

Whatever else he was to the citizens who'd placed him in office, Karl Lundergaard was the town crier. Harlan Blackthorne's reputation had made it to Minnesota.

Caspar entered the car square on the end of the last sour note. He bowed to Mrs. Blackthorne and rotated a shoulder toward the rear of the train. I holstered the revolver, not too tightly to slow its retrieval, and followed him through the dining car, sleeper coach, and caboose. That elaborately plain wooden box hadn't budged an inch, in spite of all the grades we'd climbed and descended and joints we'd bumped over; the man inside was as impossible to dislodge from his current place as he'd been from the bench.

We stepped out onto the vestibule, where a circus barker awaited us. Barely five feet, with the chest of a puffer pigeon, a straw boater pushed back from his bald forehead, window-pane suit, and gray kid gaiters on his shiny shoes, he stood with his thumbs hooked inside the armholes of his waistcoat and spoke in a baritone so deep I felt the tingling in my feet.

"Marshal Murdock? *The Weekly Democrat.* Welcome to our city."

I decided he managed that timbre through the counterweight of his moustaches, great swooping ginger-colored things that supported his jowls like flying buttresses.

"Deputy," I corrected. "Do I call you Mr. Democrat or what?"

"I ask your pardon. On the Lord's day I'm apt to forget my business manners. Eli Ferris: Publisher, editor-in-chief, staff reporter, founder of the firm, and keeper of the cistern. I understand you are accompanying the great jurist's mortal remains to their eternal resting place in Delaware."

"Right so far."

"May I speak to the Widow Blackthorne? My female readers in particular would be interested in reviewing the Judge's colorful career through the perspective of his lifelong partner and confidante."

"She's unavailable."

He released an armhole to smooth the fertile growth on his lip, stroking his thumb straight out in both directions from the center. "I assure you I have no intention of disturbing her in her hour of grief, but to lift some of the burden by way of giving her the opportunity to share her memories with those of her own persuasion."

"She drew her share from the well of spiritual comfort at Grace Lutheran this morning."

"Perhaps, if the lady herself were to decline this request in person—"

I hooked my own thumbs inside my belt, spreading my

coat and exposing the butt of the weapon in its scabbard. "Mr. Ferris, this conversation is ended."

"I cannot accept that, sir. I've already ordered this week's front page struck from the chase. When a man of Blackthorne's stature, alive or dead, visits our peaceful hamlet, the event quite outstrips even a visit from a hot-air balloon."

I'd started to take hold of his elbow and steer him toward the steps. I stopped with my hand in midair.

"Did you say hot-air balloon?"

NINETEEN

——

When **Ferris scowled,** the tips of his moustaches nearly touched under his chin.

"Yes, and it was damnably inconsiderate of them to take off again before word could reach me. The biggest local story my journal has had since Eric Gunderson's mill burned down with him inside, and I had to build it on the testimony of witnesses other than myself."

"With all due respect to the late Mr. Gunderson, when did the balloon come through?"

"This morning, before dawn; too dark even to describe the colors of the silk. It touched ground square in the middle of John Engles' potato patch and was gone within the quarter-hour. John's got as much English as I have Norwegian, so I had to piece together his account with an old phrase book and the help of my idiot printer's devil, who's as ignorant in one language as the other."

"Did Engles speak with anyone aboard?"

"D'ye think my luck changed in that regard? Unless the pilot or whatever he calls himself flew here straight from Skagerrak, I couldn't quote so much as a sneeze."

"Did anyone get off?"

"If he did, it was before Engles scrambled out of his night-shirt and into his overalls. It was the whoosh of the hot air the contraption let out to come down rousted him out of dreams of Viking plunder."

"Where can I find Engles?"

"Refilling his Sunday-scoured soul with fresh sin down at Finlay's general mercantile. The town's dry, but Finlay's back room's as wet as the Red River." He groomed his facial growth once again. "This interview's commenced to run backwards. How's about five minutes with the Widow Blackthorne in return for my generosity?"

"That's—"

"I will speak with this man, Mr. Murdock."

Less than a week out from under the old eagle's scrutiny and I'd begun to lose my edge. I hadn't even heard the door open behind me, and there was Mrs. Blackthorne touching my elbow. I turned to meet her gaze, saw in it that she'd overheard enough of our conversation to know I needed a reason to alight from the train once again, and had provided it.

Ferris pried his hat from the back of his head, bowing deeply enough to show that his hair ended precisely where the sweatband began; a perfect tonsure. I made introductions the way the Judge had taught me and waited until the pair had retired inside before stepping down.

The band was putting away its instruments as I made my way through the small collection of residents still present on the platform. No one paid me any more attention than curiosity toward a stranger; evidently Howard Rossleigh's blood-and-thunder account of my career hadn't made it into the columns of *The Weekly Democrat*. Fame is largely a question of geography.

Finlay's store had a corner entrance that gave away the building's origins as a saloon before the bluenoses had shut it down. As usual, reform had led to secret measures. Until the do-goods find a way to erase the process from history, fermented grain will find its way down every throat that seeks it.

My own included. How the abstemious managed to gain entry to a place where the truth flows like mountain runoff, I'm not equipped to say. And I was thirsty.

A window where the legitimate goods were placed on display provided a view of a tidy space, with floors scrubbed white, a plain wooden counter, shelves of cans and galvanized buckets reaching to the ceiling, and a dress form in a corner, indicating the existence of a Mrs. Finlay, or at any event a local female partner; the whistle-stop town would scarcely tempt an entrepreneur from outside. A homemade CLOSED sign with a backward *S* hung on the door, but that would be for the tourists and those customers genuinely interested in obtaining a flannel shirt or a sack of flour.

That much was obvious to an experienced tracker like me. At the base of the porch a trail ran around the side of the building, worn three inches deep by the tread of many a thirsty visitor.

The sun was just this side of noon, and shining full on a back porch next to a full rain barrel breeding algae and wigglers on its surface; Finlay's attention to his shelves appeared not to extend beyond the public room. A screen door hung at enough of an angle to invite newly minted mosquitoes to shake the scum off their wings and drink their fill from the clientele. I peered through the screen, but I couldn't make out anything beyond the rusty mesh.

That wasn't true from the other side. I had my hand raised to rap on the frame when the door swung open, forcing me to backpedal to keep it from turning my face into a Belgian waffle. The man holding the handle stood on a disintegrating thresh- old with a butcher knife in his other hand. He wasn't wearing an apron, so he didn't seem to have been cutting meat.

"A man dressed good as you ought to know his letters," he said. "The store's closed."

"This coat?" I spread it, exposing the revolver butt yet again. "I got it from Monkey Ward; but then I guess I'd need to know my letters to order it, so your point's made. I thought the sign was just a suggestion. Somebody told me I could come here to cut the dust."

"Who was that?"

He wasn't much taller than Ferris the newspaperman, but the similarity came to a dead end there. He had a long yellow close-scraped face and combed his pale hair straight out in every direction from the crown in a thatch; it looked like a dandelion in bloom. The sleeves of his faded blue flannel shirt were rolled tight past his elbows, exposing hairless forearms as thick as half-grown stoats. The long muscle that ran up the right leapt and twitched as he flexed his fingers around the handle of the butcher knife.

"I didn't catch his name," I said.

"Folks hereabouts don't take to sharing their affairs with every drifter. If it's supplies or provisions you're after, come round tomorrow. I'm passing the Lord's day with friends."

"He said he was a friend of John Engles'. Is he here?"

"You got a bum steer, stranger. All of Engles' friends are

right here in this room." He started to draw the door shut, but I was standing in its path. The knife came up a notch. It looked at home in his grip. I calculated the odds of drawing the Deane-Adams without losing the use of that arm. I didn't like the numbers.

From behind him, one of his friends let out a belch that started low and rose to a crack, like "The Star-Spangled Banner." Someone who might have been the perpetrator said, "Aw, let him in, Floyd. I'm sick of looking at the same old faces."

He had a singsong accent, plainly Scandinavian. That was encouraging, if it wasn't Swedish or Danish or Finnish. If Ferris were any kind of journalist he'd have come here for his interpreter when the balloon landed.

Finlay didn't look to be wavering. Moving slowly and using the hand opposite my holster, I fished out my poke and shook it so that the coins scraped against each other inside.

That seemed to be the password. He executed a practiced maneuver, reversing the knife's handle from underhand to overhand, and thrust it under his wide leather belt.

"Two bits a pour."

"How long's the pour?"

He stepped aside, still holding the screen door, and canted his now-empty palm toward a shelf built from packing crates, lined with pint canning jars. I plucked loose a cartwheel dollar and dropped it into the palm. "That should get me started."

TWENTY

—

It **was a** small room and close, papered with catalogue pages advertising plows, ladies' undergarments, and Dr. Strauss' Miracle Wormer, cut into crooked aisles by freestanding shelves of canning jars, mismatched wooden chairs, buckets of lard, and a coffee grinder with embossed wheels big enough to support a locomotive. A great hickory stump served as a cutting-table (the cleaver was sunk deep as Excalibur), next to a pickle barrel with a red-and-white enamel dipper hanging from a nail in the wall above it. The lid was off, telegraphing the smell of pure grain alcohol as far as ten feet. Two fresh sides of venison dangled from a single rope slung over a rafter, divided down the spine, probably by the same knife Finlay had under his belt; *The Weekly Democrat* had been spread under it to catch the drips. The red meat laddered by ribs had a pungent earthy odor peculiar to freshly butchered wild game.

The still was a model of its type. It was self-contained for indoor operation, with a fire burning in the base of a boiler from a steam engine and stovepipe to draw the smoke out through the back wall. Fifteen yards of coiled copper pipe dripped crystal-clear liquid into a bucket at the rate of a drop a minute; a man could mesmerize himself watching it quiver on the nozzle and guessing the point at which it would let go and plop into the bucket. Notwithstanding the pace, some three inches of two hundred-proof skullbuster had accumulated in the bottom in the time I was there; enough to turn a meeting of the St. Sebastian Committee to Prevent Social Injustice into a fandango.

The proprietor demonstrated a surprising sense of parlor etiquette, introducing each of the men who sat in the chairs: "Oskar Newmunster, Gilmer Gurst, John Engles. You got a name besides the one you come in with?"

They stared up at me, cradling their jars as if I might snatch them away. Their faces had been left out in the rain to swell and turn gray, then in the sun to crack and curl, then in the snow to bite their noses and cheeks with frost, in patches the color of white lead. They ran to a common age. A citified easterner would reckon it at fifty or better, but I'd spent enough time in open country to subtract as much as twenty years from that; they'd look no older at eighty, if the work didn't take them first. They wore church coats in as good condition as they could be kept in that part of the world, except for Engles', which needed brushing and had for some time; plainly, he was the one without a wife. I pegged Newmunster as the man who'd cast his vote in my favor; his pale blue eyes were friendly, and there was something about the cast of his features that suggested Norway and none of its neighbors. This was one of those inexplicable visceral assumptions that held up in Blackthorne's quarters but not his court.

The name I came up with was another.

"Howard Rossleigh. I'm with the Montana Press Association."

Finlay grunted. "You're a piece off your territory."

"I'm on special assignment for the Hearst Press, to travel the country and report on items overlooked by the competition."

Lies came to me like ticks to a dog; telling them was a talent I'd brought with me to law enforcement, and one less thing for Blackthorne to tutor me in. There were advantages to being raised by a Montana trapper who spun yarns through the winter in order to ravel them for whoever'd listen come spring.

Newmunster showed a gold incisor. "You came to the right place, then. This is just about the overlookedest town east of anywhere and west of no place at all. Even the balloons don't set down long enough to steal dust. Ask old Engels here." He pointed the rim of his canning jar at the unbrushed man seated to his left, dour-looking and short-waisted, with a pair of legs stretched out in front of him that gave the impression he'd been split more than halfway up his length. He'd been staring down into his own jar, but now he perked up at the sound of his name, like an old bird dog. His friend assaulted him with a singsong jabber, waving his vessel my way.

Engels' demeanor changed. Seeing himself the object of a stranger's attention, he brightened three shades and answered in the same tongue, slopping liquid from his jar as he outlined a great circle with his hands, accompanying the gesture with a hoarse gust of air that approximated the whoosh a silken bag makes when the pilot manipulates it to expel heated air for the descent.

None of this was new to me; I'd seen and heard lighter-than-air craft land. But I put on a face as excited as the potato farmer's, took out my memorandum book and pencil, and made some doodles on a blank page. I stopped him once to get the spelling of his name, which when Newmunster translated the question made him puff out his chest.

Gilmer Gurst, a man with sails for ears and hair curling colorless as seaweed over his collar, was less interested, as was Finlay, clearing their throats impatiently at intervals. They'd heard the story more than once; but I prevented interruption by exchanging a quarter for a jar of Purgatory. The contents were so transparent they didn't distort the shape of my hand when I peered through the glass, but they left a flaming trail of coal oil down my throat and reverberated like a bass drum when they hit the floor of my stomach. I sipped slowly after that, in order not to miss a syllable of what Engels had to report:

> ME: *Was anyone aboard besides the man who operated the balloon?*
> ENGELS (through Newmunster): Ja, *two.*
> ME: *What did they look like?*
> ENGELS: *One was taller than the other.*
> ME: *But what did they* look *like? Dark, fair, clean-shaven, bearded? (Rossleigh's horsecollar whiskers were memorable.)*

The farmer shrugged, got irritated when I pressed him.

> ENGELS: *It was dark and they were too far away.*
> ME: *Tell me more about the balloon. How big was it? (Seen one, seen them all; but I was losing him with too many questions about what were to him mundane details. I sped up my scribbling while he described the damn thing all over again using his hands. It got a little bigger with each repetition.)*
> ME: *Did anyone get off?*

ENGELS: Ja, *but they were already across the patch when I got there.*

ME: *They? You mean both men got out together?*

Here Engles looked at Newmunster and said something that wasn't directed to me.

"What?" I asked his friend.

Gold glinted. "He asked me if 'they' means the same thing in Montana as it does in Minnesota."

It took me a moment to work that out: There were three in the balloon, including the pilot.

The farmer was sure the passengers hadn't left with the craft.

I asked him where I could find his potato patch. Again an aside to Newmunster.

"He's afraid you'll trample his plants. That contraption already—"

"Tell him I'll pay for any damage."

Engels nodded when this was translated. Then his face brightened again and he lifted his jar. I didn't need an interpreter for that. I paid Finlay for another round. By the time I took my leave they were ready to elect me mayor.

Beatrice Blackthorne looked up from her knitting. "*Two* men? Are you sure?"

"One taller than the other. Rossleigh's six feet."

"Are you not leaping to a conclusion?"

"There's still no sign of *The Javelin*. Short of hopping a balloon, I can't think of another way he'd have gotten here ahead of us. What are the odds of one landing in this burg the same day? And what happened to those passengers? You saw how much interest we attracted. To stay out of sight in a town this size, unaccustomed as it is to traffic from outside, they must be up to something."

Her nose wrinkled. "Have you been drinking on the Sabbath?"

So much for grain alcohol having no odor on the breath. "If Finlay had been serving lemonade, I'd still be there waiting for light to break."

"My just desserts, I suppose, for inquiring into your methods. I swore never to do so, and my marriage was happy in consequence. What can you hope to learn by visiting the potato patch?"

"Tracks," I said, "leading in the general direction of the livery where someone took a potshot at me."

"You will proceed with caution, of course. His aim may improve next time."

"It would have to go some to do that. If that bullet was meant for my heart, we wouldn't be talking." I tugged loose my necktie. "How did things go with Young Pulitzer?"

"Young—? Oh, you mean Mr. Ferris. It became obvious early on he wanted to bring his readers to tears. I accommodated him; at some length, of course. I assumed you needed the time without interruption. I must say, bringing up old memories—" Her gaze dropped to her basket and her fingers resumed working. "Well, one cannot live in the past, can one?"

"I've been thinking the same thing this whole trip."

I changed from my town clothes to dungarees, my duck coat, and stout boots, and followed a pair of wagon ruts from town to a plot with a narrow two-story unpainted house and a barn three times its size with what looked like a fresh coat of whitewash tinted rusty red from the iron oxide the farmer mixed in to seal the source of his livelihood. The place was rich with the odor of freshly turned earth and manure, and the rich brown soil preserved footprints like wet clay. Engels' waffle-patterned soles and the half-circle of his plow team's shoes were easy to separate from a set of side-by-side tracks leading toward town from a square indentation some four feet in diameter—the print of the gondola—near the center of the field. A pair of square-toed town shoes were spaced far enough apart to suggest the long stride of someone like Rossleigh, but there were places where the gait appeared to have shortened, probably to allow the hiker's smaller companion to catch up.

The second set belonged to a pair of significantly smaller feet, which bore closer study. These shoes were pointed, with circular punctures left by the heels. They were narrower than those worn by men who depended on such heels to grip their stirrups when they rode; men like me. And that fact turned every theory I'd brought to that piece of ground square on its head.

III

THE COURT
ADJOURNS

TWENTY-ONE

———

"Taters."

"What?"

In the spring of '77 it seemed I was always asking Bear Anderson to repeat himself. At seven feet and two hundred fifty pounds, he was accustomed to working out every muscle except the ones that controlled his power of speech. What passed for oral communication was a deep, grinding murmur that sounded more like a grizzly chasing tenderfeet in its dreams.

"I bet I dug enough taters out of this patch to cover the mountain top to bottom ten times. Funny thing, though."

I waited. You did a lot of waiting when you were in the mountain man's company, unless you belonged to the Salish Indian tribe. The mere appearance of a brave within lunging distance turned him into a whirling frenzy; whether his bowie or his fist struck first depended on what side of him his despised enemy was standing; the power of the blow itself determined whether the Indian was still breathing when his scalp took leave of his skull.

I lost patience and prompted, "Funny thing?"

"I'm blowed if I can remember ever eating a single one of them spuds."

We were standing at the time in an acre of Bitterroot Range country grown over with vines that no longer bore fruit, on the edge of which still stood the gaunt blackened timbers of the cabin he'd grown up in, fifteen years after he'd set fire to it with his parents' massacred corpses inside. His father, a Norwegian (like most of the population of the Minnesota settlement the Blackthorne train had stopped in), had felled trees for his pay and scrabbled in the dirt to feed his family when the money ran short. Whether the renegade Salish had resented the cutting or the plowing had long since ceased to draw the curiosity of the slain couple's neighbors; they were more interested in the body count their son continued to exact from the tribe.

His legend—for it was that—didn't shake me. Of all the men who rode for Blackthorne, I was the only one who'd grown up in the territory. I couldn't remember a spring that didn't come with a new horror story that had played out during the months of short days and long nights; husbands and wives alike lost their footing on reality when they were snowed in for weeks on end, raced each other for the axe or cleaver, and finished as often as not in a dead heat. Tales of cannibalism weren't just inventions to put the children to bed on time. The community looked forward to details of the occasional incest as a respite from blood and gore.

What rocked me to my heels was that Bear's long one-man

war against an entire people, much of it involving hand-to-hand combat with knives and tomahawks (and a strangling that had consumed most of an hour and three hundred yards down a mountainside) wasn't the first thing on his mind when we visited the scene of his parents' murder. It was potatoes.

A week or so later, the big man had dangled from the scaffold in Helena—on the second try, after his weight snapped the first rope. I was the one who put him there (after persuasion that had nearly left me behind with the Andersons' potatoes) by the Judge's orders in response to a demand from the Bureau of Indian Affairs in pursuit of a peace treaty with Chief Two Sisters, hereditary leader of the Salish Nation, inaccurately referred to by the eastern press as the Flatheads.

"Spit it out, Deputy," Blackthorne said. "I can't have an officer of this court moping about like a wallflower at a cotillion."

"Give me time, Your Honor. I knew Anderson since he wasn't any bigger than a heifer. We camped out together when my father was on his trapline and his was away jacking timber. He taught me how to use a bowie without slicing up my hand." If he hadn't, the last part of our story would have had a different ending.

"I'm aware of your shared history. Why did you think I selected you to bring him in? Anyone else who got close enough wound up decorating the man's belt with his topknot. You didn't complain when I gave you the assignment."

"The plan then was to try him, in order to avoid an Indian war. I didn't know it would play out the way it did."

"Neither did that butcher I made the mistake of promoting from turnkey to hangman. He thought he found a bargain in South American hemp. Dollarhyde, his successor, used the

East Indian variety exclusively; consequently he was never obliged to hang a man more than once. You must have known you were condemning your old friend to execution. The Flatheads would have settled for nothing less."

"I was drunk on the spirit of the chase."

"An appropriate metaphor. A morning after is part of the transaction. You'll get over it. Hangovers don't last."

The Judge was wrong there. I never ate another potato, and to this day I can't spend any time in a patch without thinking I should have stepped aside for someone else.

An ostrich-shaped silhouette stood on the edge of John Engles' patch, with the town at its back. That bulge halfway between its head and its long thin bowed legs could belong only to the local guardian of the law. Karl Lundergaard stood in the shade of a straw hat with a flop brim, carrying a single-barreled shotgun in the crook of one arm, broken at the breech, the way a bird hunter does to avoid shooting his pointer dog before it can flush out supper. He might have been just out hunting, at that; in that long-tamed country, a peace officer carrying a weapon out in the open was getting to be as rare as a balloon sighting.

I made a beckoning gesture. He hesitated, then started my way, mincing between the green sprouts on corns and bunions. The man was tailor-made for collaring boys chucking rocks through store windows. As a manhunter he'd be worse than no law at all.

"I heard you talked to Engels," he said when he reached me. His breath chugged. He'd hiked all of a hundred yards from his parlor.

"Nothing gets past you, I guess."

I waited for him to take the bait and look down, but whatever he was using for eyes back in those swags of liverish flesh remained level with mine. Finally I pointed at the turned earth at my feet. He stared at my finger for a moment, the way a dog does when you try to direct its attention to a bone. Then his head tilted forward, wallowing in his chins.

"Town shoes, both pairs," I said. "It isn't every day you see tracks like that in a potato patch. The arches are too high for walking any distance."

"It *is* Sunday. Folks get out their best for church, and cut cross lots to shorten the hike."

"These start in the middle of the field, where the balloon set down."

He nodded. Somehow I had the impression he'd already come to the same conclusion. Arguing was a habit he'd gotten into to avoid serving the responsibilities of his office.

"That would explain it. A ride in the sky, I'd put on spats for a thing like that."

"An eagle-eye like you would know if there were any new faces around, all decked out for civilization."

"Maybe so. Then again maybe not, if they didn't spend much time here."

He'd got his breathing under control, but that didn't entirely account for the satisfaction that had crept into his tone. He was looking at me now; so far as I could tell.

I let out air. "Play your hand, Lundergaard. I've got a bellyful of the Devil's tea and no head for guessing."

"Merle Thompson owns the livery. After you and I talked I dropped by his house, neighborlike, to tell him somebody busted into the stable. I went with him to check the place out. I don't guess you noticed two horses was missing."

"I was too busy ducking lead to search the place for a list of the inventory."

"I figured as much. Anyway they were two of the best animals in his care, owned by a couple of our most respected citizens, so he's all hot to track 'em down. I ain't Dan'l Boone, so I thought of you straight off."

"No one was ever Daniel Boone, including Daniel Boone. I can't go haring off after horse thieves and leave Mrs. Blackthorne unprotected. You'll have to handle it yourself, Marshal."

"This ain't Tombstone or Dodge City. We don't get but one felony in six months. Two in one day—if what happened to you wasn't some yonker's prank—in the same place raises the question that we're both of us interested in the same folks. Two sets of tracks in John Engles' field settles the thing for me."

"For me, too. But my job's to get the widow and what's left of her husband to Delaware before he starts to turn. I've been shot at before, so I don't place as much value on my hide as your respected citizens do on their horseflesh."

The inside of a cheek got chewed. The action caved in that side of his face. I decided his skull ended just south of the bridge of his nose. "She won't be any better protected if I arrest you for violating the town ordinance against purchasing hard liquor."

"Finlay won't like that. I'd have to name him as the man who supplied it. You'd have to shut him down and turn all his loyal customers out into the street. When do you come up for re-election?"

"I asked for your help as a sworn officer of the law. You turned me down. I don't reckon anybody'll squawk if I jail you for obstruction of justice."

"I hate to disappoint you again, but the Judge won't keep while I wait for you to build a jail."

He slammed shut the breech of the shotgun.

A dime novel I read—hell, all of them—placed a lot of store in watching a man's eyes for the instant when he was going to act. None of those writers had ever stood face-to-face with an armed opponent. Eyes don't kill; hands do. I was watching the hand at the end of the arm Karl Lundegaard had rested his scattergun on, open at the breech so it wouldn't discharge by accident when he stepped in a gopher hole. The tendon extending from his wrist to the base of his thumb twitched just before he palmed up the forepiece of the weapon, closing the breech and bringing the hammer into position to strike the shell in the chamber; I saw the skin stretch, because I was watching for it.

He found himself looking down the muzzle of the Deane-Adams.

I said, "Now what would the good citizens of this community think if their guardian of justice and a federal officer blew each other to bits in the middle of a potato patch?"

He gnawed on his other cheek, considering the odds. Finally it occurred to him they didn't fall on the side of a part-time lawman. He lowered the shotgun.

I let the revolver drop to my side. "Common theft falls under your jurisdiction," I said. "If it's your hide you're worried about—"

"I ain't worried about that!"

"Sure you are; think I'm not? The lady had only a belly gun

the last time I looked. At any range that puts you one-on-one with her accomplice." I didn't add how good the accomplice was at range.

What I'd said shook him to the soles of his big clumsy feet. "Lady?"

TWENTY-TWO

—

I scuffed the edge of one of the smaller tracks with the toe of my boot. "That belongs to a woman's pump. If it's the woman I'm thinking of—and another in this story seems too much like coincidence—when it comes to Remingtons, my hunch is she's a better hand with a typewriter than a firearm. Her name is Betsy Pike; she's a reporter for the Hearst press."

"Betsy Pike? Now I know you're spinning one."

"It's an alias. She endorses her bank draughts with the name Pamela Green. That is, if she didn't make that one up, too. Everything she told me is open to closer inspection since I came across her dainty footsteps in this plot of dirt. But maybe she did grow up on a farm in Ohio, at that. It can't be easy to walk in unturned earth in heels without stumbling unless you're used to the terrain."

I told him about our conversation aboard *The Javelin*. I'd already gone over the simultaneous disappearance of our conductor and Howard Rossleigh, but I touched on it again. There was no reason to fill him in, except he was in a way a colleague, and he struck me as honest.

Then he swept his hand at a gnat buzzing around his head, forgetting he was holding a shotgun and clouting himself on the temple.

Rubbing the spot with his other hand: "Why'd a reporter throw in with somebody who'd attack a railroad conductor?"

"Why would another reporter attack a railroad conductor? I'll ask him when I find him; or you will. Right now my responsibility is with Mrs. Blackthorne and that box in the caboose.

"We'll be in St. Paul tonight," I went on. "She has an appointment with a lawyer there, so we'll have to stay over until tomorrow. Why don't you round up a party and see if you can find out where those stolen horses went? You can wire me there with what you find out."

"You mean a posse?"

It might have been my imagination, but it seemed to me the unmade bed of his face brightened at the use of the word.

Somehow, lacking speech, Caspar had managed to persuade a merchant to open his store on Sunday and sell him some tinned fruit and a sack of baking powder, and when I got back to the train it smelled of warm peach cobbler. Mrs. Blackthorne and I spent the entire conversation over the treat commending the chef's skill. After we shook our heads at the offer of a third helping, I brought her up to date.

"She must be under Rossleigh's heel," the widow said. "I do

not entertain the possibility that a woman would willingly assist in such a crime."

"Your late husband sentenced a woman to hang for stabbing her own infant daughter to death in her cradle."

"I remember the decision. He agonized about it for days, and for nothing. The sentence was commuted to life by order of the U.S. Congress. I wrote a letter to President Garfield protesting the misplaced chivalry, but that man Guiteau shot him before he could respond. In any case that woman was deranged. Everything you have told me about the Green woman indicates she is as sane as you or I."

"In 'eighty-nine I arrested a buffalo hider for crushing his partners' skulls with a shovel. He was convinced they were demons. The jury acquitted him on the grounds of lunacy and he was committed to a madhouse in Washington State, where he did such a good job pretending to be sane the staff released him. A week later he set fire to a hospital. I never found out if he thought the doctors and nurses there were demons or if it was the patients, because he was burned up along with them. Just because someone's crazy doesn't mean he isn't clever enough to hide it."

She shook her head. "You have been too long at what you do. Your dinner-table talk is revolting."

"I've had complaints. I think Pamela Green has her head screwed on tight enough and then some. If I'm right, you and I have been thinking about this all wrong, believing Rossleigh to be the one in charge. Whichever one of us is the target, getting rid of the man in charge of our train didn't require any thought. Conductors do more than punch tickets. Young as ours was, he'd be trained in dealing with unwanted passengers, hoboes and such. Face-to-face fighting is more a male specialty, and if anything went wrong, the brains behind the operation remained safe away from the scene."

"You misjudge the feminine advantage. A man accustomed to expelling tramps might hesitate in the presence of a woman, especially one dressed as daintily as you described. As you pointed out so graphically, the shedding of blood is not restricted to the male."

"She could also be a fair hand with a gun; but it wasn't her in the livery."

"You said it was a small round, such as hers would fire."

"I did. It was. But the shoes don't signify. Whoever took that shot might have climbed into the loft wearing ladies' pumps, but couldn't have scrambled out the opening afterward; there wasn't time to avoid snapping an ankle. If she'd brought along a pair more practical, why didn't she have them on when she walked across that field? I've met them both, and she was the one who struck me as the more dangerous thinker."

She looked out the window, at the smoke drifting from the locomotive. "The woman who established your opinion of the fair sex must have been Jezebel incarnate."

I gave that some consideration. Then it was my turn to shake my head.

"Not quite as wicked, maybe, but smarter. In the end, the original schemed herself into getting thrown out a window. But it's Pamela Green we're talking about now. She was smart enough anyway to let her partner take all the risks while she waits for her chance."

"But at what? Or should I say at whom?"

"Right now only she knows the answer to that one. Meanwhile we'll continue east." I rang a note off my dish with my fork. "At least we don't have to go looking for them."

"Because I am a helpless old woman and cannot be left alone."

"You're wrong, and not just about being helpless. We don't have to go looking for them because they'll come looking for us. As long as we stay aboard this train, we're rolling bait."

TWENTY-THREE

Our talk might have continued, but then the wind freshened, snatching away the smoke. Afternoon sunlight carved deep hollows under her eyes. By neither word nor signal would she have pleaded for rest. I was about to excuse myself when the car shifted under a heavy set of feet.

Our engineer announced himself before we saw him; he smelled like an unswept chimney. When he peeled off his cap, it left a precise line where the soot that blackened his face ended. Pink scalp glistened in a way that seemed vaguely obscene. He was holding his turnip watch in his other hand, face up on the palm like a compass.

"Beg pardon, missus, but there's a freight due through here in half an hour. We best get going if we don't want to be stuck on a siding."

Mrs. Blackthhorne read the answer on my face, nodded.

I was strung too tight to sit in the chair car. I went back to the caboose—automatically touching my hat as I passed the coffin—and went out onto the vestibule, gripping the rear railing as the little cluster of buildings that stood in for civilization in that part of Minnesota shrank into the horizon. The steeple of Grace Lutheran Church was the last to withdraw. It seemed a week since the widow and I had attended services there.

It was farther east than I'd been in years; long enough anyway to see the changes that had taken place while I was doing the same thing I'd been doing since I left cowpunching; and there'd be no going back to that even if I'd cared to. The big ranches that seemed they'd go on raising cattle for a hundred years were cut up into dirt farms. The straight Western Union posts had been replaced by rune-shaped telephone poles, the wires that had carried news of Lee's surrender, Custer's massacre, and the Oklahoma land rush now borrowing a ride below sundry jabber. A plume of dust caught my eye—were any stagecoaches still running?—but it turned out to be chasing a steam thresher across a plowed field. A freight wagon stopped at a crossing, its bed piled with gas pipes intended for some town prosperous enough to turn up its nose at coal-oil lamps. Most of the horseflesh we'd seen since leaving Helena was hitched to buggies and buckboards. In a few years a man sitting a saddle would be a sight worth noting. Someone had told me there was an Oldsmobile dealership in St. Louis. The West had gone and gotten itself young while I was busy getting old.

It was well past dark when we rolled into Minneapolis, and it had changed most of all. On my last trip I could have drunk a whiskey in all its saloons—they called them beergardens there—and still walked a straight line. Now I couldn't visit half of them dead sober without wearing my heels all the way to my ankles; and they weren't the most plentiful establishments in the city. Long after Creede and Cheyenne had rolled up their awnings, the windows of the German village I remembered were as lit up as Saturday night in Barbary, with loiterers in straw boaters smoking on every corner.

There was no sign of a brass band; one benefit of not keeping Prosecutor Callaway apprised of last night's stopover.

A pudgy kid in a uniform with the tunic buttoned wrong stepped onto the platform as the train whooshed to a stop and I knew on the instant he was there for me. There was no conductor to set up the step-stool, so I hopped down from the coach, startling the messenger.

"I'm Murdock," I said. "Is that for me?"

He looked down at the yellow envelope in his hand as if I'd just conjured it up. Then he nodded and raised it. I took it and slipped a nickel into the same palm. He touched the visor of his cap with the fist he'd closed around it and got out of my life.

> REMAINS YOUR CONDUCTOR FOUND
> MISSOURI RIVER STOP WIRE ME BISMARCK
> FOR DETAILS
>
> HOSEA JOHNSTON
> DEPUTY US MARSHAL

I was dithering over whether to share the news with Mrs. Blackthorne until I knew more when she made the decision for me, addressing me from the door of the coach. I reached up the telegram. She read it at arm's length.

"That settles it, then," she said. "Howard Rossleigh killed the man."

"I can't say yes or no until I get the rest; but the simplest answer is usually the right one."

She consulted the tiny gold watch pinned to the lapel of her traveling suit. "I am meeting Lawyer Morton tomorrow in St. Paul. In order for me to prepare for whatever he has to discuss, it would be a significant relief if I were to spend one night away from this train. It is not one of your responsibilities, but do you suppose you could arrange accommodations?"

I asked the station agent to recommend a hotel.

He glanced up over the tops of his hornrims. "The Railway Arms is just a five-minute walk."

"Now recommend one with hot water and no ticks."

"Mandan's the best in town." A pair of mud-colored eyes evaluated my duck coat with its colony of cinder burns. "It ain't cheap."

I put my forearms on his counter and leaned in close. "I'm Jay Gould's bodyguard. Don't let it get around."

I got directions, and stopped at a post office on the way to wire Deputy Johnston, directing him to respond at that office. I didn't know the name; but he would be assigned to whatever federal court claimed jurisdiction over the Dakotas.

The Mandan Hotel, a pile of sandstone guarded by noble savages carved across the lintel, opened to me at the service of a red-whiskered Irishman dressed in a bone vest, breechclout, fringed leggings, and four turkey feathers stuck stiff as pickets in a gaudy headband. His feet were broad and flat in machine-made moccasins and he had to wrestle a feathered lance into his other hand in order to open the brassbound door. Inside, terra-cotta tiles with thunderbirds and other totemlike symbols embossed on them stretched for a quarter acre. I waited half a beat for a second brave to escort me to the desk before I realized it was carved from cedar and holding a fistful of unsmokeable cigars.

All this was, I supposed, intended as a kind of post-apology to the Mandan tribe of Minnesota and the Dakotas, an entire Indian nation wiped out by a smallpox epidemic borne by white visitors. Imperfect prints of George Catlin's paintings of early Indians decorated the walls of the foyer in redwood frames carved into primitive designs the actual primitives wouldn't have recognized. The foyer swarmed with Indians, except for the guests lounging in the club chairs.

The clerk behind the desk gave my clothes the same evil eye I'd gotten from the station agent. When he craned his neck to see I wasn't carrying a bag, the waxed points of his wiry moustache twitched. I was all out of drollery, so before he could summon Geronimo from outside the door to show me out at lance point I palmed my star and told him I wanted to book two adjoining rooms in the name of Beatrice Blackthorne.

The Judge's name had legs enough to reach that far across the continent. The clerk retracted his moustache-tips, spun a ledger the size of a family Bible around on its swivel, dipped a horsehair pen in a pot of ink, and handed it to me with all the ceremony of a tanktown mayor presenting President Arthur with the keys to the city.

I signed for both of us and accepted two keys with copper tags embossed with numbers. "Suites four-twelve and four-fourteen, sir. I trust they meet with your approval."

I told him it was Mrs. Blackthorne's approval he had to be concerned about, and left to fetch her.

Nearing the train station, I heard a steam whistle. A small locomotive was slowing from the west. Hearst's *Javelin* had caught up with us once again. I wondered if Pamela Green and

Howard Rossleigh had stepped down from their stolen mounts to board it or if they'd ridden on ahead and waited for it to whisk them away from another encounter; and if they intended this one to be more final than the last.

TWENTY-FOUR

———

The Unholy Alliance wasn't likely to attempt anything in as public a place as the Minneapolis train station, but just to be safe I made sure Mrs. Blackthorne was secure (she looked up from the valise she was packing with a quizzical expression; I shrugged unfeigned ignorance), then searched the train from end to end; not overlooking the Judge's coffin.

Using a pinch bar the late conductor had kept probably to inspect suspicious crates of cargo, I pried off the lid, wondering what the Penalty was for disturbing the dead. If it was chains, I was in for a fortune in scrap iron.

It was no stowaway tucked away in the satin lining. The Benedictine Brothers hadn't skimped on embalming agent, but the man in the box had sunken in on himself in places, most noticeably the mouth, the lips pleated in the absence of teeth. If anything he looked even more Satanic than he had in life.

"Beg pardon, Your Honor." I replaced the lid and tapped the nails back into their holes with the blunt end of the bar. Then I retired to the dining car to spread out the flimsy pages I'd brought back with me.

Evidently the latest Panic hadn't reached North Dakota. I'd stopped again at the post office on my way back, not really expecting a reply yet from Hosea Johnston, but he must have had something prepared, and whoever he answered to was no skinflint: I found a wire four pages long waiting for me at the telegraph desk, written in a code different from the one Judge Blackthorne had invented, but similar enough in approach for me to work it out at the table with the help of my Bible, memorandum book, and stump of pencil while the widow was packing for her overnight stay.

The marshals' service wasn't any more devout than the Department of War, but the King James Bible was more easily obtainable than even *Ben Hur*, and the numbered chapters and passages remained constant throughout every edition. Notwithstanding the quaintness of the language, the Word, rearranged of course, expressed itself clearly in every state and territory of the Union, if you knew the key.

In sum, the message informed me that our conductor, one Christopher Stedman, had been found bobbing in a backwater of the Missouri by a fisherman, and had been identified by the rags of his uniform and what the water had left of an employee card in his wallet. Fish and bloat had gotten to him, making him unrecognizable to even a close relative, but his build matched the description that had been sent out by the railroad. The cause of death was undetermined (and likely would remain so, given what the coroner had to work with). I was satisfied that he'd been stabbed; strangling doesn't spill blood, and even if I'd missed hearing a gunshot, that method was risky. Anyone who managed to commit murder aboard a train carrying a deputy United States marshal and carry away his victim's corpse without anyone the wiser wasn't the careless sort.

I returned to the sleeper, where my fellow passenger was bent over a lower berth, buckling the straps on a portmanteau. I told her the latest, including the arrival of *The Javelin*.

She addressed the last part first. "Do you think Rossleigh and Green are aboard?"

"They had enough of a head start after the livery to have beaten us here on horseback if they rode hard. My guess is they lay low and signaled the Hearst train to pick them up, then turned loose the horses."

"In which case we passed them on our way here."

"Even if we thought that was what they had in mind, we couldn't be looking out the windows all the time, and anyway a train is an easy thing to hide from. One way or the other, they're close."

"Should we recruit the local authorities?"

"They've been too smart so far to try anything in as busy a place as this. I could be wrong, but if we clutter up the landscape with badges, they'll go back underground. I don't know about you, ma'am, but I've grown weary of waiting while they make all the decisions."

She slid her bag to the side and sat on the edge of the berth, her hands folded in her lap. From the side she'd look like a picture of a painting I'd seen of the artist's mother, only a good deal less placid. "Mr. Murdock, I suspect you are hatching a plan."

"Sitting on it for now. I'll tell you more when the shell cracks. Thanks to Johnston's telegram, we know now what we only suspected before, that our conductor is dead and that Rossleigh and Green aren't shy about using as much force as they need to get the job done."

"That is hardly progress, as we were in little doubt of the facts. I would breathe easier if we had some inkling as to what the job is."

I retrieved my own valise, as tarnished and travel-worn as I was, from the upper bunk where I kept it, and set it on the floor. I'd been living out of it since Montana; unpacking and repacking were luxuries I'd learned to live without long before I came to the court. "I'm hoping it's me, because I'm used to that. But they threw away their best chance at our last stop, when they missed my heart by four feet. My money's still on Rossleigh for that, but he had plenty of time to aim. What either of them hopes to gain from a game of cat-and-mouse has me up a tree."

"Perhaps it is I they hope to rattle."

"In which case, Mrs. Blackthorne, they don't know you from the man in the moon."

"I have always fancied it is a woman," she said. "Always faithful, but impossible to predict as to where and when she will choose to appear."

A bellman—refreshingly dressed in ordinary brass buttons and dog-dish cap, no feathers—materialized in the terra-cotta lobby to take our bags, but I waved him off and climbed the broad carpeted stairs beside my companion, carrying my valise and her portmanteau.

Chesterfield lamps set gold threads twinkling in the runner on the fourth-floor hallway. I had both keys; I unlocked 412 first.

"I'm registered in four-fourteen," she said.

"I haven't forgotten to open the lady's door first. We're switching rooms."

"Ah. Of course."

More and more I knew why the Judge had chosen her for his partner. Few things needed explaining to her.

There wasn't a copper's worth of difference between the two rooms. Each had a Brussels rug, one green, the other burgundy, a four-poster heaped with quilts, pillows, and bolsters and requiring a walnut sort of mounting-block to climb onto, marble washstand, chiffonier, writing desk, swags of velvet on the windows, and prints in frames, one set of Washington crossing the Delaware, studying a map at Valley Forge, saying farewell to his troops, and taking the oath of office, another of Grecian women bathing in chaste gowns. The Indian motif didn't extend to the upper floors. Someone had probably decided the guests would sleep better if they weren't surrounded by tomahawks.

I handed her key to her, placed her bag on her bed, and left, pausing in the hallway to hear the latch sliding into the jamb. In 414 I threw my valise onto the upholstered bench at the foot of the bed and extracted the flask of Old Gideon I traveled with. I paused in the midst of drawing the cork, then rammed it home and put it back between my folded shirts. Whether Rossleigh and Green fell for the most transparent ruse in the world, or anticipated it and made their assault on the room Mrs. Blackthorne was actually sleeping in, I was better off leaving the fruit of the grain alone.

I opened the connecting door on my side the better to hear what was going on in the adjoining room, took off my hat, and opened the Good Book to a random page:

I will meet them as a bear that is bereaved of her whelps,
and will rend the caul of their heart, and there I will
devour them like a lion; the wild beast shall tear them.

It wasn't a passage I'd have chosen to retire on, and it led to things I wouldn't have chosen to dream. And it was from the book of Hosea.

I slapped the book shut. There was nothing in it that would guide me out of this limbo. A hunch took me. I'd learned the hard way never to dismiss one. They didn't always turn out, but when they didn't there was no harm in following them, and nothing but when they did and I failed.

For the first time in my life I found a use for all the frippery the better hotels supplied to justify their confiscatory rates. The bolster stood in for a human torso, the various sizes of cushions and pillows for the head and limbs. With the counterpane pulled up over the approximation I achieved, anyone entering the room on the prod would have taken it for a sleeping figure. The trick was as old as Plymouth Rock, and just as sturdy. I turned down the lamp on the nightstand just enough to simulate repose and provide illumination for the opposite, pulled a Second Empire chair over to the door connecting to 412, and sat, tipping it back far enough to rest against the wall, but too far to avoid falling on my back if I didn't stay alert enough to maintain balance, with the Deane-Adams resting in my hand across my lap. That was the theory, anyway. A body at rest finds a way to stay at rest against most odds, but the wakeful mind can take only so many precautions against its enemy, fatigue.

If Rossleigh and Green fell for the second-oldest trick since the Pilgrims landed, expecting to take Mrs. Blackthorne in the bed that had been assigned to her by the Mandan Hotel, I was in the best position to bring this drama to an end. All I had to do was stay awake.

Nothing new in that. I'd stayed vertical as long as I had by years of training, stringing out sleep two hours one night, six the next, and so on, until I could squeeze eight hours' rest into fifteen minutes with my eyes closed. But that's a young man's game, and without thinking about it, the absence of the Judge had eroded my inner senses to the work of his Court.

The nearly constant movement since Helena had worn away at my attempts at sleep. The sudden stop on solid earth must have its effect. I lost touch with the world minutes after I sat; and dreamt, of things past and done and beyond reversing.

TWENTY-FIVE

In the fall of 1881, Harlan A. Blackthorne's bailiff was a frail ghost of a man named Platter, whose thick, black-rimmed spectacles were the only things that kept his face from blending into a whitewashed wall. He expired of a disease of the blood eighteen months after taking the post, but in that time he killed a shackled prisoner making a break for a window on the way into the courtroom and crippled another as he charged the bench intending to strangle the Judge with his chains; that one climbed the steps of the scaffold on crutches. Platter was as fast and accurate with either of his .36 Navy Colts as he was quiet in his speech. I had to rise from my chair outside court in order to hear what he was saying.

"His Honor won't be calling you today, Deputy."

I glanced at the Regulator clock clonking on the wall opposite. "He's adjourning early?"

"In a manner of speaking. He collapsed during proceedings and has been taken to his home."

The Blackthornes' houseman, a former Deer Lodge Penitentiary trustee who called himself William Red Lion, met me at the door.

"Doctor's with him." He closed it in my face.

I went from there to Chicago Joe's, which dispensed all the latest local news along with liquor, cards, and women. The gents who bucked the tiger at the faro table knew everything worth knowing except how to satisfy their landlords. For the price of a beer I found out the Judge had been unconscious for an undetermined amount of time before the prosecutor appealed for a ruling on procedure and failed to get the usual lightning-quick answer. The case was rape and murder, and I'd been summoned to testify as one of the arresting officers. I'd been left outside to go over my testimony while Platter and a teamster who'd offered his services from the gallery carried the Judge out the back. Since it was unprecedented for a jurist in that bailiwick to exit the room without a formal adjournment, the opposing lawyers had spent twenty minutes discussing the legality of dismissing the principals without consent from the bench, and if so, which of them should be the one to do it. Platter took the responsibility upon his return. The last I heard, that irregularity was still making its way through the appeals process.

"My blasted heart," Blackthorne told me when he was permitted to entertain visitors. "It isn't enough that I'm attacked in the Congress and assaulted by the defendants it's my duty to try; now one of my own organs has decided to throw in with them."

It was the first time I'd been in his bedroom. He shared a sitting room with his wife, but this place was exclusively his. I

wasn't surprised to see that the gimcrack that existed
throughout the rest of the house was entirely absent. His bed
was large but plain, with a tall oak headboard curved like a
tombstone, and shared the modest space with a dry-sink, a
chest of drawers, a maple wardrobe, and a nightstand holding
up a coal-oil lamp, his teeth in a glass of what looked like water
but might as easily have been grain alcohol, and a copy of the
territorial penal code the size of a paving block; even his bed-
time reading tied into the demands of his office. In the weak
light filtered through gauze curtains, his face was nearly as
pale as the oversize pillow Mrs. Blackthorne had provided for
him to sit up against, and his eyes behind the pince-nez seemed
twice their normal size, but his hair and pointed whiskers were
as chimney-broom black as ever, and the hands resting on
the pile of court papers in his lap were brawny and corded.
He wore his old purple dressing-gown and a plain nightshirt
with the same solid dignity of his judicial robes.

I drew a straight chair next to the bed and smiled sympathy. "Your heart's not the only culprit. I talked to your doctor.
Seventy hours a week working without a break makes you an
accomplice, along with that high-toned tanglefoot you drink
by the case."

"That charlatan. The only thing duller than his wit is his
needles. The Hippocratic oath means as much to him as the
one you swore when I made the mistake of recommending you
to Dockerty."

U.S. Marshal Argus Dockerty had been in office when I
joined the court. Only the marshal, a presidential appointee,
had the authority to hire deputies; but even that early in his
tenure, Blackthorne had usurped the privilege. He handpicked
the men who rode for him, forcing them upon the tin-star
politicians who came and went with each administration. That

high-handed action came up every time Washington debated a budget for the western territories; one of the reasons he got away with such things was the list of grievances was so long it would take more than an entire session of Congress to discuss it in detail.

"I keep my oath when it doesn't get in the way of the job," I said.

"It's up to me to say what the job is, Deputy."

"If you're having second thoughts, I've got a standing offer from Chicago Joe to throw drunks out of her place. The pay's the same, but the hours are fixed, and when they aim at me they're too far gone to hit anything important."

"Twenty a month and all the Old Pepper you can drink. I can see you settling into that." He almost sneered; but he'd have needed his teeth for that.

"You're forgetting the hostesses."

Worldly though he was, the old man had a Puritan streak that prevented him from pursuing that line of conversation. His expression struggled between rebuke and retreat before a spasm of some kind settled the point.

"I'm told I'll be six months recovering," he said. "That's time sufficient for this territory to revert to its savage origins. I will be back in harness significantly sooner, even if it means convening court in this room."

"You'll need to tear out two walls to accommodate the spectators. There aren't seats enough downtown as it is."

I didn't intend flattery, but he appeared placated. His was the biggest show in the territory, and he took pride in the fact. When a capital case was under examination, there wasn't a vacancy to be found that side of Butte.

"How is Chet Arthur's fair-haired boy getting along?"

The president had appointed a surrogate to fill the hole in

the judiciary. Dennis Kennedy had graduated Harvard twenty-second out of a class of twenty-five and had spent most of his time after clearing the bar running errands for a justice of the Supreme Court, including lining up escorts for celebrations of State; the Washington Press Corps referred to him as "the U.S. Procurer General."

I hesitated before answering. The last thing I needed on my conscience was another seizure. On the other hand, I'd never withheld official information from the Judge.

"The jury hung this morning on Ballinger."

He'd pled cases before assuming the bench, so his poker expression remained in place. Only someone who'd been in close contact on many occasions would notice the nerve jumping in his left cheek.

Lug Ballinger was the man Blackthorne had been trying at the time of his attack. When it came to molesting women, arson for profit, digging up corpses for the gold in their teeth, and selling alcohol unfit for human consumption to Indians, he'd been in and out of federal custody more times than the courthouse rat. This time I'd arrested him on the evidence of the widow of the copper miner he'd decapitated with the victim's own shovel, then taken the woman by force. Her testimony on the stand had been emotional but courageous, and its effect on the jury visible.

When at last he spoke, Blackthorne's tone was calm. "You gave evidence?"

"In pieces. Kennedy sustained the defense's objections more times during my spell than you did all this year."

"I hope you're exaggerating. Uninterrupted, the Honorable Lucius Venable could turn back Great Falls with his Latin."

"I heard it came to twenty pages in the transcript. Seemed like more."

"What about the instructions?"

I was silent another moment, then drew the folded front page of the *Daily Herald* from my pocket and passed it across the counterpane. He snapped it open, found a foothold for his spectacles, and read the dense column in which Kennedy's charges to the jury were quoted in full.

When all the evidence had been given and the opposing counsels have delivered their summations, it was the jurist's responsibility to explain the various degrees of the felonies involved, repeat admonitions to ignore portions of testimony that had been stricken from the record, and provide a translation of legal argot into plain English. I'd sat through Kennedy's instructions, and it hadn't taken training in law to recognize the confusion on the faces of the jurors. If I'd been seated on that panel, knowing everything I knew about the case, I'd have been at a loss whether to convict or acquit based on that advice.

Blackthorne read to the end of the column without tipping his hand. Then he sat back, closing his eyes. A pattern of tiny blue veins showed on his lids. I'd never seen them before. They looked as thin and fragile as moth's wings. "You're dismissed, Deputy. I'll rest now."

I got up and let myself out. I had the door almost closed behind me when I heard the harsh brittle noise of newsprint being crumpled into a ball; and I knew it wouldn't be half a year before the Judge returned to his responsibilities.

During Dennis Kennedy's tenure, the U.S. federal court with jurisdiction over the territory of Montana ran up a record nine hung juries, costing taxpayers three hundred thousand dollars in retrial fees and freeing three previously convicted felons when the prosecution elected not to press its case a second time. Blackthorne set his own record when he picked up the gavel again after less than six weeks in recovery, against his doctor's strenuous objections. (Although he modified them when his patient promised to honor a regimen of daily exercise. The Judge bought a billiards table.) One of James A. Garfield's first official acts as president was to appoint Kennedy to a cabinet position.

I heard a floorboard shift, and leapt fifteen years and a thousand miles to a hotel room in Minneapolis in less than a second. By the time someone tapped on the connecting door I was on my feet, the chair I'd been sitting on spun to the side, and the Deane-Adams gripped tight in my fist.

"Mr. Murdock?"

In the instant it struck me she'd never called my name questioningly; and I wasn't sure at first it *was* Mrs. Blackthorne. The voice was pitched low, almost but not quite a murmur, which unlike a whisper seldom travels beyond the earshot of he who was intended to hear it. If it belonged to her, both the tentative nature and the register might have been signals that someone was standing close, most likely with a weapon at hand, expecting me to open the door to her if to no one else.

I didn't answer, but stepped away, pivoting silently on the ball of my foot, and reached my free hand to the lamp on the nightstand, turning it out. Reversing directions, I took up a position on the side of the door opposite the hinges with my back to the wall and palmed the knob at arm's length. Intruders generally expect a cautious victim to choose the side closest to the hinges, for the leverage it offered them, to jerk the door open hoping to catch the threat by surprise; but I had nowhere to go and all the time there was. I turned the knob slowly, and when the latch let go gave it a gentle pull and withdrew my hand, letting the door drift into the room under its own weight.

It moved at glacier pace. A gap lit by the lamp in the next room widened excruciatingly slow, like the minute hand on a clock.

The light reflected off a white temple. I planted the muzzle of my revolver against it and drew back the hammer. In the stillness of the room the crackle was deafening.

"Mr. Murdock!"

This time it was a gasp. It was the first one I'd heard from that source, and with sound reason. I'd come within a hair's width of sending Beatrice Blackthorne back into the arms of her dead husband.

TWENTY-SIX

—

The Mandan Hotel saw to all its guests' comforts. On a corner of the writing desk in my room glittered four crystal goblets on snow-white linen lining a silver tray. Once I had Mrs. Blackthorne settled into my armchair, I uncorked the travel flask and charged two glasses with healthy draughts of the amber-tinted stuff the better butlers used to thin the mahogany stain on their masters' dinner tables. When she stuck out a hand, palm forward in a signal to stop, I pressed one into it and curled her fingers around it. She followed the gesture with her other hand, as if her fingers were chilled and it was a steaming cup of chocolate; but she didn't drink.

"Doctors prescribe brandy in cases of shock," I said. "I imagine they don't lack for nervous patients. This is whiskey, but it delivers the goods without counting the candles on its birthday cake."

She smiled wanly. "I am aware of the medicinal properties

of spirits, young man. We spent the first three years of our marriage in my parents' old smokehouse, which my father used to make his own beer. Harlan did not propose to me for my fortune or social standing."

"The odds are he never stuck a pistol to your head either." I tossed my dummy out from under the covers and sat on the edge of the mattress, cradling my own glass. "I'm sorry again. If it's me they're after, using you to get through the door seemed the obvious choice."

"Vanity." She sipped, coloring her cheeks, and lowered the glass to her lap. She wore the same nightclothes I'd seen her wear that one time in the sleeper: flannel robe, gray nightgown, and suede slippers, once a deep maroon but now faded to a grayish pink. On this occasion I saw some remnants of black among the silver and white in her plaited hair, and thought of the raven-haired bride Harlan A. Blackthorne, Esquire, had carried across the threshold of that newlyweds' cottage, rank as it was with cured ham and green beer. "You are fixed on the notion that you are the object of our enemies' scheme. Is it that you wish to spare me from panic for myself, or do you hold your own life in so high regard that no others' could match its worth?"

I'd turned the lamp back up after rescuing her from her near faint (*near* being the key word; she'd staggered a step when I lowered my gun, catching herself even as I reached for her arm). Now I held up my glass, admiring the way the facets broke the light into splinters of red, blue, and yellow, like sunrise through a stained-glass window. "This stuff is better than I remembered. It must have been the rocking it got on the train."

"Stuff. We assign to inebriating agents qualities we possess already; rapid recovery from a startlement is one. Great age will do for you as it did for me—provided you attain it. The closer one comes to the Abyss, the less frightening is the prospect of being hastened over the edge. I have done all that someone in my position was expected to do. The only chore left is to wait. I abhor waiting."

"Not everyone shares your view. I've seen women older than you—men, too—hanging by their eyelashes to that last inch between them and the—" I paused. "Why Abyss, by the way? I took you for a committed Christian, serene in the promise of bliss eternal."

"Why, because I continue to observe Sunday services even when a thing like a cross-country journey to bury the remains of my husband would seem to excuse me? A habit established over many years can be mindless, and its point lost. I have hopes, of course, of an afterlife in a place better than this."

"Hope and faith are different things."

"I was not speaking carelessly. My faith is in storage. I placed it there when I watched my father slip from this world, first by inches, then by yards, until he no longer recognized me or remembered the forty years he worked in a tannery, retiring as a foreman. Where is the soul when a body is committed to the earth bereft of its past?"

"I can't picture that happening to you."

"*That* is hope. Most of mine were fulfilled when the man I spent my life with passed to his reward with all his properties still in place. I had feared the worst ever since the first attack on his heart; wondering if the next would take aim at his mind. I am not the soldier you think, to stand courageously by and watch a brilliant man turn first into a child, then into a dumb brute."

I drank. She was right, as usual. It was just Old Gideon after all; nothing more miraculous than the pleasant heat it wired to the extremities. Her strength came from inside. "You just wiped away any fear I might have had that a bullet would take me before my time."

"I doubt you ever dwelt upon that." She took another sip, placed her glass on the nightstand, and gripped the swan-shaped arms of the chair. "I thank you for the restorative. There is no reason to forgive you for taking proper precautions. He was correct in his choice of companions for this journey."

The Judge was *he* again; as if nothing of an intimate nature had passed between us. I shifted my weight onto the balls of my feet, stopping her in mid-motion. "Why did you knock on the door?"

She shook her head. "Foolishness. I had a nightmare. The details are unimportant, but I wished not to fall back asleep immediately and take up where I left off. I selfishly decided to disturb your sleep, in return for a few moments of aimless conversation. Perhaps I brought the shock upon myself, as punishment for ungenerous behavior." She made a dry sound in her throat. "That, you see, is faith."

"*That* is bearing false witness."

She stopped in mid-rise, brows raised. "Even in such pious terms, to call someone a liar is an insult and an abomination."

"The insult is in the lie," I said. "You forgot I'm a fellow believer. It's the Judge's fault. He schooled me in the Bible, just as he forced me to study the classics so I wouldn't embarrass his court, and sent me to Texas in a clerical collar. As a Christian himself, he should have known I'd come back changed. And so I borrowed from Exodus and accuse you of bearing false witness." I plucked the tattered volume from the nightstand where I'd placed it facedown and handed it to her, open to the page I'd been reading.

"This is Hosea," she said, "not Exodus. Surely you selected

the book before retiring, asking divine reason why it was Hosea Johnston who brought you the news of the conductor."

I accepted the return of the Bible and closed it, letting it rest in my lap. "I won't waste time convincing you it was random. It may mean nothing, probably doesn't; I can't afford to be besotted. Any old book with a loose binding will fall open to odd passages; it's rare in *this* book not to have some kind of significance for the reader. I only wanted to show you I don't use it just to dress up the place."

"I never for one moment—"

"That nightmare story is a lie, Mrs. Blackthorne. You might have been awakened by one, but you could have avoided taking it up again just by picking up your own Bible and reading until you were drowsy. Do I need to go into your room to prove you keep it by the bed also?"

Hers was a difficult face to read, but I'd had daily opportunity to study it, as I had Holy Writ and Charles Lamb's essays. I saw her color change, and spotted the moment when she decided anger was pointless. She sat back—not quite touching the rear cushion; she hadn't drifted so far from Eastern civilization—and retrieved her glass.

"I am past worrying about the improprieties," she said. "Do not think that is the reason for my dissembling. The mind that would see only filth in an old woman wishing to enter a young man's bedroom—"

"I'm not a young man."

"—is not worth concern. I do detest displaying weakness, and even more admitting to it. The simple fact of the matter is I cannot accustom myself to sleeping alone."

I stared. I hadn't been prepared for that.

"It's been days. You must have had *some* sleep."

"I would not dignify it with that name. The details of

funeral arrangements, preparation for this journey, the meddling of the press, and the difficulty of resting on a train in motion gave me little opportunity to reflect upon the emptiness at my side. This is the first night I felt truly alone, and realized this is how it will be for the rest of my life."

"But you kept separate rooms."

"That was our little conceit, for the sake of the servants. The more conscientious they are, the stodgier. Sharing a bed is unseemly for a man and wife of our years. Harlan was always careful to go into his room upon rising and muss the covers in his bed. It amused him, I think, to humor the sanctimony of the staff."

Her smile grew distant. The picture of the Judge in his nightshirt, scrunching up his sheets like a little boy who'd sneaked into his parents' bed, was less disturbing to her than to me. She shook loose of it.

"Perhaps it's that we're in a hotel. As I was turning down the bed tonight, I remembered that Harlan and I spent six nights in such rooms traveling to and from Fort Lincoln, to help send off an old crony of Harlan's, who was retiring from the military. That was our last trip together. Suddenly the thought of climbing under those covers chilled me to the bone. I know these are the imbecilic fears of a woman in her dotage, and yet—"

I remembered the glass I was holding in my own lap, next to the Bible. I drained it, set it and the book down on the table, and slid over on the counterpane, spreading it open on her side. "I should warn you, I snore when I've been drinking."

When she smiled this time she showed an enviable set of teeth, patently her own. "As do I. I have that on the good authority of my late husband." She got up from the chair, leaving her robe draped across it.

TWENTY-SEVEN

I lay awake a long time, not because of the situation, but from instinct. For lack of heat or space I'd been forced to share beds with cowpunchers, buffalo runners, Indian braves, and strangers whose very gender was open to question; a couple of horses and a mule, if you counted stables. When circumstances crowded close, most of the touchstones of civilization were cast overboard; sleeping with the boss's widow was no more scandal than cuddling up to a goat for warmth.

The goat in this case being me.

Evidently it was no challenge to Mrs. Blackthorne. She'd been under the covers, her back turned toward me, less than five minutes when her even breathing told me she slept.

With her husband she'd left the seat of a victorious Union for one of the least-settled territories in a West still bleeding from civil war, crossing two thousand miles of wild prairie, mountains, and arid waste, under conditions that only a few years later were the stuff of fable. The Transcontinental Railroad was still in pieces, the great Indian nations poised to challenge an army torn and weary of battle, the landscape itself armored, fanged, and thorned. It had attacked them from above and below, often at once. They'd bunked in the holds of flatboats, slept under wagons, and fled from sandstorms and blizzards and Cheyenne dog soldiers in dugouts alive with ants, rats, and worse. If the Judge hadn't exaggerated—and that was one flaw he didn't exhibit—they'd escaped starvation snowed in in an empty farmhouse by boiling wallpaper for the flour paste. Lying next to a half-broke lawman with a bad conscience in a plush hotel was nothing to stay awake for.

I remained dressed except for coat and boots; again, not from any sense of decency as to be prepared, with the Deane-Adams loose in my hand down by my side where I lay on top of the spread. At my request, my bedmate had turned the lamp back down low, but not out. My eyes were best left adjusted to some light in case quick action was necessary.

Everything about the situation said it wouldn't be. A frontal assault on a gilded establishment in a city as settled as Minneapolis defied all logic.

If you think that way, Page, I can't use you. It places all the ammunition in the hands of the enemy. Anarchy thrives on illogical behavior. Here in Helena we fight it with laws and structure. Out in the field they'll kill you faster than a bullet.

He had all the answers, the Judge had.

The son of a bitch.

I was playing three-card monte in my head: The ace of spades was on the left last time; this time would it be on the right, in the center, or left again? If on the right twice in succession, what were the odds the dealer would gamble on turning it up in the same spot a third time? I'd patted myself on the back for my cleverness in switching rooms with the widow, but if she wasn't the target, had I stacked the odds even higher against her by putting her in the room I'd been assigned? And now, whether I'd been right or wrong, what did both of us in one room do to the danger?

The puzzle was unsolvable, and should have been enough in itself to keep me awake.

It wasn't. I slid into a black pool of molasses.

The window burst. Shards shredded the curtains and the lamp's glass chimney popped and tipped over with a tinkle. The crash of the report itself came as an afterthought.

Gallantry is the first casualty of armed conflict. Clasping my revolver tight to my waist, I rolled left and shoved with all my weight. Mrs. Blackthorne, who was just stirring awake, resisted out of impulse, but I had the element of surprise and my momentum was greater. She slid over the edge of the mattress and landed on the floor, hard enough to jar the still-burning lamp off its base. I was prepared for that. I caught it with my free hand and set it right, blowing out the flame in the same motion. The room went black.

I was still rolling. I landed on top of her; the air left her lungs with a *woof*. More glass pattered down onto my back, simultaneous with the sound of the second shot and then a third.

After that came a lull. I used it to think.

The room was in the front of the building, too well lit by the gas lamp on the corner to scale without attracting attention. The bullet had to have entered more or less parallel with the floor to break the chimney, and there was no reason to think the others came from any other gun; at least I hoped so. Then the shooter had to be firing from directly across the street, probably from a window facing ours. Random fire is no guarantee of success; the attack would have to be followed up by a visit in person. In order to enter the room on foot, he'd have to run down several flights of stairs, cross the street, and climb three more flights past a crowd alarmed by the shots.

He wouldn't do that, any more than he'd scramble up an exposed wall in a busy city and swing in through the window.

All this raced through my mind in the second and a half after I shoved a widow out of bed, compounding the crime by crushing her with my weight. I knew who the shooter was and that he had a partner, probably already in the building. The last was my advantage, because it ruled out the window as a source of further attack.

Unless.

Unless the partner had decided to wait for the shooter to catch up and pinch us between two fronts. That added a card to the game, hiking the odds against us even higher.

Mrs. Blackthorne was fully awake now. I could feel the rapid-fire beating of her heart through my own chest. I twisted away, releasing a shower of broken glass to the floor and giving her room to lever herself onto a hip and into a sitting position with her back against the nightstand. My eyes were adjusting to the conditions; just enough gaslight trickled through the torn curtains to fall dead white on her face. Her plait had come undone and her mouth hung open, but not to scream. She was breathing heavily through it, drawing in great gusts of air to refill her chest. When she'd gathered enough to speak, I stuck out my free hand and pressed it against her mouth.

Then I winked.

I still don't know why, but it seemed to calm her. She nodded jerkily, and when I took away the hand flung the loose hair out of her eyes and drew her knees into her chest, wrapping the hem of her gown around her bare feet. That cleared the way for me to kneel beside the bed and prop my elbows on the mattress, holding the Deane-Adams in both hands with the muzzle in line with the door to the hallway.

The room had a fireplace with an iron surround that served as an echo chamber to the ugly bronze clock parsing out the seconds on the mantel. Every few strokes the ticking matched the thump of the pulse in my temples. It was dangerously mesmeric. When a door panel split with the noise of a mortar blast, the shock sent my first shot wide. That might have been the end of us both, but the door was built of stout oak and took a second blow from the battering ram—it turned out to be one of the heavy majolica smoking stands set yards apart along the hallway—to open a gap wide enough to thrust the little belly gun through and snap a slug past my right ear, too close for relief.

I recognized the pistol, an over-and-under Marston derringer; I couldn't see the pearl grips, but I knew they were there.

Not that identifying it affected my own aim.

I put two more through the shattered panel. They'd both have been on the money, except the first hit the target, knocking it out of the line of fire and throwing off the second; but one was all it took.

TWENTY-EIGHT

———

Minneapolis was not Karl Lundergaard's sleepy hamlet. The first shots had awakened most of the guests on our floor, and by the time the last finished echoing, the hotel was swarming with policemen in blue serge and brass. One, a burly middle thirties with black longhorn handlebars, a stiff helmet, and a badge the size of a tea-saucer pinned to his tunic, stood at the end of the hallway near the stairway landing with one arm wrapped around the waist of a struggling figure, the other a deep-bellied revolver pointed my way. The scene looked like an illustration on the front page of *The Police Gazette*.

I stopped; of course. I stretched my gun hand out to the side, let the Deane-Adams drop, and raised both hands to shoulder height.

"I'm a federal officer," I said.

"We'll come to that. And who's this?" His accent was Midwestern, flat as a griddle and as filled with emotion.

This was slightly built in a loose corduroy coat, plain trousers, child's-size brogans, and shapeless hat crushed down over the ears. As it squirmed to break free of that girderlike arm, the coat fell open, exposing a red stain on the pale blue fabric underneath, an inch above the waistline, spreading and changing shape in pace with the slowing of her resistance.

It was a her. A sudden spasm jerked her head hard against the officer's chest, knocking the hat askew and releasing a fall of hair, haloed red in the light of the Chesterfield lamp overhead. Her foot kicked the derringer lying on the carpet runner into a spin. The grips gleamed bone-white.

I said, "She says her name's Pamela Green, but she goes by Betsy Pike, a name you might have read in the papers. You'll see it on the obituary page if you don't get her to a doctor quick."

His gaze flickered down, then back up. For an instant there was confusion in it. Then a squad of men dressed as he boiled up from the stairwell, fisting revolvers and sticks, and he bundled the woman into the arms of the one closest. "Get her into the wagon. St. John's." To a dumbfounded face: "The hospital, man!"

He returned his attention to me, his hogleg trained on my sternum.

"Do not shoot!"

I didn't turn to see who was speaking. I knew the voice, its tone steady even in the wake of what she'd just been through.

"Beatrice Blackthorne, Officer. My husband was Judge Harlan A. Blackthorne; you may perhaps have heard of him.

This man is Page Murdock, a deputy United States Marshal assigned to his court. I am under his protection."

I took advantage of his hesitation, lowering one hand to fish the star from my pocket between two fingers. It was half the size of the shield he wore, but he must have seen one in the past. He lowered his weapon and seated the hammer.

St. John's was a Catholic hospital. The nurses wore the black-and-white livery of the Church, moving along the whitewashed corridors in swift silence, the hems of their skirts gliding across the scoured floorboards as if they had bicycles hidden underneath. Novices, dressed less severely, carried brimming bedpans—the ammonia stench lingered moments after they passed—and pushed buckets and mops on carts, the rubber wheels squeaking. Under it all was a constant powerful throbbing of mysterious source. If I closed my eyes I might still be aboard the train.

In a waiting room down the hall from where a team operated on Pamela Green, I talked. My audience was the big policeman—a sergeant named McGraw—a party in street clothes with a bitter-lemon face who introduced himself as Lieutenant Pohl, then went silent for most of the interview, and a female stenographer in plain gray wool, a chignon the size of a sombrero, and the first monocle I'd ever seen worn by a woman. The black ribbon attached to her lapel swayed in rhythm with the gravity pen racing across the writing-block in her lap. Mrs. Blackthorne had been excused from the session to dress in room 414 of the Mandan with a police guard outside the door and patrols circling the building at street level. Another detail had been assigned to keep reporters away from the waiting room. Within minutes of the shooting, the Blackthorne funeral party was as well-known as a visit from the president.

"You've said nothing about why the Green woman and this Rossleigh want your hide," McGraw said when I stopped talking to drink water from a plain glass. We were all seated on the kind of hard wooden bench such establishments provide to add physical agony to the ordeal of visiting the sick.

"You'll have to ask Miss Green, if she makes it. I'm not even sure it's my hide they're after. The kind of enemies the Judge made might have carried their grudge to his widow. Is there any news on Rossleigh?"

"The building across the street belongs to a land office, which closes at six. Someone broke the lock on a back door and our boys found a window open on the fourth floor, almost directly across from the busted one in the room you, um, shared with Mrs. Blackthorne."

He stopped long enough for me to provide an explanation. I watched him without blinking.

He moved on without a lick of embarrassment. "They smelt burnt powder. He had enough time to clear out after the shooting. We'll get him, if the description you gave is any good."

"If he hasn't shaved off that beard, he's not as smart as I think he is."

"Our men know about such things as ears and noses and eye color," Pohl put in. His speech was thick with gutturals. "A razor is no defense against our methods. We keep the peace with our eyes and our brains, not our trigger fingers."

I looked at McGraw. "Whose brother-in-law is he?"

The handlebars spread. "Uncle, actually. Married to the deputy chief's aunt."

"You're insubordinate!"

"Stating a fact. Sir."

Pohl stuck a long skinny finger at the stenographer. "Strike all that!"

She drew several lines and waited for more.

I said, "How long has she been in there?"

The sergeant undid a brass button with a practiced flip and extracted a steel watch from his tunic. "Close on two hours. If I had to guess, I'd say the heavy door took some of the edge off—"

The lieutenant, who was sitting opposite the door to the operating room, stirred. We stood to face a tall, stoop-shouldered man of fifty or so wearing an apron that reached to his knees. "Which one of you is Murdock?"

I said I was. He removed a pair of wire-rimmed spectacles with fogged lenses, skewering me with intense blue eyes. "She asked for you. I was told it was you—"

I said it was. He shook his head. "You made a thorough job of it. We extracted the bullet, but we got the bleeding stopped too late. Pointless to move her to the recovery room. She hasn't much time."

"We're going in too," said the lieutenant.

"You are not."

He glared at the doctor. "This is a local—"

McGraw touched his arm. "Not much time, the man said."

The sour face darkened. He thumped my chest with one of his talons. "You'll report what's said. To us only."

"You, the Widow Blackthorne, and Grover Cleveland."

The doctor held the door for me. I went through alone.

The room was bright with light from electric bulbs. That explained the vibration in the walls. It came by way of a combustion generator chugging away in the basement. The atmosphere was oppressively hot, and the smell of alcohol and carbolic made my head swim. Beneath it prowled something more earthen: unpleasant, familiar, impossible to ignore. The patient lay on a leather-upholstered table under a thin sheet. Her face was bleached of all color and she looked as small as a child. Her chest rose and fell in uneven fits. Her breath whistled. I hadn't seen her hair down before; it looked darker in that merciless glare, and clung wetly to her forehead and bare shoulders. A straw hamper on the floor next to the bed was heaped with bloodstained gauze; that was where the baser odor was coming from. A wheeled cart bore matching stains on the snowy linen cloth that covered it, from the disarranged instruments deposited there, shining steel slick with crimson.

I'd seen far worse, under moldy canvas in muck-covered battlefields where sluicing down a pine table with a bucket of water was as sterile as things got, with wounded men lying outside on stretchers beside corpses, amputated arms and legs stacked in cords awaiting burial, and everywhere the stench of sweat, offal, and vomit; but that had been many years ago, and if anything age had made me more sensitive to the consequences of keeping the peace; ludicrous phrase that it was. I'd violated it as much as anyone had that night.

When I came in she was staring at the ceiling. Now her eyes moved my way. I could almost hear them scraping in their sockets. Dark purple indentations showed beneath them. It stirred something disturbing; a memory I couldn't quite retrieve.

She spoke barely above a whisper. I had to bend down and place my ear almost to her lips.

"You don't know who I am, do you?"

It came out a word at a time, at a dollar apiece based on the amount of effort that went into the process.

I thought for a moment she didn't recognize me. "You're Pamela Green; Betsy Pike to your readers. You told me, remember?"

"And you believed it."

"I couldn't come up with a reason not to."

"Fool!" The heat of her breath gusted in my ear. "I'm neither. My mother gave me her name. She had no other to give. My name is Pamela Bower. I'm Colleen Bower's daughter."

TWENTY-NINE

A hand stroked my cheek; the fingers were too soft to have dealt so many cards from the wrong side of the deck.

"I hope it doesn't scar," Colleen said in her purring contralto. "You're mean-looking enough without that."

"If that's an apology, keep it to yourself. You weren't so worried when you tried to put a hole in me."

Colleen Bower—*Mrs.* Colleen Bower, not that I ever had the pleasure of meeting Mr. Bower, if he'd existed—levered herself up onto her elbow, letting the rose-colored sheet fall to her breasts. In Breen, Montana Territory, in 1879—a boomtown, with no shortage of good-looking women working in their own ways to make a strike, they were as firm as any around.

Whenever she studied something as closely as she did my face, the gold specks in her eyes spun like snowflakes. "I didn't know who or what you were then. All I knew was I came back to my room to find a strange man in it, searching through my things."

"Would it have made any difference?"

"I doubt it. But that early in our acquaintance, if the bullet had flown true, I wouldn't have felt as bad as I would now."

"That's not the same as saying you wouldn't try to backshoot me again."

She'd buried at least one husband by that time, and would again: In '84 or '85, *Harper's Weekly* published a cover piece on her under the title "The Widow Never Weeps," saddling her with five tragic marriages and strongly implying that she'd had a direct hand in two of them and had brought the rest about through guile. She sued the publication for libel and won a large award; but the forbidden tree had borne fruit. Half a dozen "Lady Bluebeard" pamphlets sprouted within months from presses in the East. She couldn't afford to take them all to court. My favorite was wrapped in red-and-yellow paper with an illustration of a woman in a black corset on the front, confiscated from a prisoner awaiting trial in the Helena jail. The woman's hourglass figure resembled the mark on the abdomen of a black widow spider.

"You rugged bulls make too much of backshooting," Colleen said. "If I made a practice of meeting my armed enemies face-to-face on the street, like they do in sensational novels, I'd have been looking at the earth from the other side years ago."

"How *many* years?"

"A gentleman doesn't ask such things of a lady."

"Those two strangers aside, how long have you been tinhorning?"

"How long have you been marshaling?"

"Not long enough to know better than to turn my back to an open door. I should thank you for the lesson."

When she smiled, she paid tribute to the latest dental science in the East. Her hand crept round behind my neck. "I have so much more to teach."

She did, too. I was still learning, and she'd been in the ground for months.

A lot of towns had come and gone since that one. All that was left of Breen was a scatter of grown-over stones and a human bone or two, dug up by coyotes; but while it lasted, it was as hide-side out a place as any man ever saw back when cattle paid better than silver. The town had colluded with the Judge to back me into a corner, taking over as city marshal in the absence by death of my predecessor. I'd tamed it, more or less, but time had done the job more thoroughly, and all the blood that had spilled was like water drained away through fissures in the clay. Colleen had thrived on the sulfurous blend of brothels, black powder, and bad men; it had drawn me in the course of my work; and so our circles had overlapped again and again. But she was as dead as Breen. And so would her daughter be soon.

If it was her daughter. One thing they had in common was a knack for polishing a lie until it glittered like gold.

I straightened to get a better look at the woman dying on the operating table. Her forehead was high and white, her build slight but gently formed, and I'd seen the curve of one of her calves, slim and firm. Now that I thought of it, when she'd had full use of her voice its low musical scale had vexed me, like an idea that kept slipping out of reach.

"Her eyes were blue."

Pamela met my gaze. When she spoke, her breathing was almost normal.

"Yours aren't."

THIRTY

——

The tea room on the ground floor of the Mandan Hotel was decorated in shades of mauve and dusty pink, with cabbage roses the size of acorn squashes on the wallpaper and a massive chandelier dripping with glass pendants. A waitress dressed like Anne Boleyn refreshed our cups from a pot on our table and drifted on to do some other work of charity. At that early hour, Beatrice Blackthorne and I shared the place with two other guests, a pair of matrons in feathers and jet chatting over their cakes.

I doctored my cup from the flask of Old Gideon. My companion touched hers with a gloved finger as I was replacing the cork. I poured a few drops into her tea.

She was dressed younger than her years, but not to the point of self-flattery. Black, of course, made of some non-reflective fabric, with a placket concealing the buttons and a hat made of the same material suggesting the prow of a ship, the brim curled up on one side and fastened with a black satin bow. It rested at a slight angle in her upswept hair. Her face, nearly seamless, showed nothing of last night's ordeal.

Mine was another matter. Everything through the small hours of this morning had revealed itself in the mirror as I was making myself presentable in 412. The room itself, cleared of debris, the shattered door panel replaced with a piece of temporary birch and the window reglazed, had recovered almost beyond noting.

"She grew up without a father, and so she blamed you."

"She says," I replied, "*said*. I don't know if I heard her right the whole time. By the end she couldn't manage so much as a whisper. She said Colleen told her on her own deathbed. That seems to be the place of choice for confessions."

"And the Bower woman never told you."

"It might not have mattered if she had. My kind of work doesn't lend itself to paternal responsibility." My voice sounded bitter even to me. I helped myself to a dram. It boiled on the way down.

"I am certain you believe that. To tell Pamela would only have deepened her resolve. Her mother has been gone a short while only. When she joined the press train assigned to Harlan's journey—from what you said, she had advantages in the area of manipulation—she was consumed with vengeance. That was why Howard Rossleigh purposely missed shooting you in the stable. She wanted you to herself—after you'd suffered sufficiently, not knowing which of us was the intended victim. She might in time have tempered her hatred with mercy, as her mother did."

"*Mercy* isn't a word I'd associate with Colleen Bower."

"We are all capable of it, even the worst of us. She spared

you the last time you were together. A daughter has a right to know where she came from, but to burden the father after so many years would be to cause unnecessary regret. Whatever she was in life, she was gallant at the close." She tasted from her cup, expressed her opinion of the adulterated brew by pushing it and the saucer away. "In Pamela's case, there would be the added resentment that you never offered her mother your support."

"Colleen supported herself on the backs of nearly every man she ever met. I was the exception."

"And that told you nothing?"

"Let's talk about something else."

"Very well. How did Pamela manage to recruit Rossleigh?"

"I didn't get the chance to ask." I had seen the moment when questions became useless. It hadn't been the first time a life had drained away before me—it always showed in the eyes, like a cloud erasing the sun—but I knew this one would stay with me to the end. "She was her mother's daughter, and Rossleigh is only a man."

"What did the police say?"

"I told them she was too far gone when I got there."

"Was that wise?"

"Not if it would help them find Rossleigh, but I don't see that it would. This way they'll divide their investigation between my possible enemies and yours. If they find out I'm the one Pamela wanted to kill, they'll hang their entire department around my neck everywhere I go. I can't do my job pulling a chain behind me."

"Yes, I'm sure that's the reason you didn't tell them."

I let that run loose and drank. She was right about the combination. I blamed the tea.

She glanced down at her lapel watch. "I have an appointment

with Nigel Morton, the attorney, in half an hour. Will you escort me?"

We hired a carriage to take us to St. Paul across the Mississippi River, which had carved a two-hundred-foot gorge, streaked black and gray with agate and red with iron. The city on the opposite bank was Minneapolis' identical twin, rife with limestone lintels and Grecian columns. The nearer we came to the cusp of a new century, the farther its architecture retreated into the ancient world.

The firm of Morton, Winslow, and Morton occupied two floors of one such building, with its name chiseled in Romanesque characters across the front. We passed through a revolving door—only the second in my experience—and followed the echoes of our footsteps to a desk on the far end of a drafty lobby. The young man seated there heard our request, unhooked a tube attached to a hose, repeated Mrs. Blackthorne's name into it, placed the tube to his ear, and replaced it on a hook.

"Room three hundred. You'll find the perpendicular railway around the corner."

This turned out to be a brass cage containing a trim young Negro in a pressed gray uniform, who worked a lever and lifted us off the ground floor with a hiss and a creaking of cables.

"How does it work?" I asked the operator.

"Hydraulics, sir. Except in the winter, when it doesn't."

A rail ran three-quarters of the way around the cage at waist height. I reached behind me and gripped it with both hands.

Gold-flecked numerals on pebbled glass identified Room 300. Inside, a female secretary—a handsome one for a change, unbespectacled and wearing a shirtwaist that hadn't been starched stiff as a plank—smiled at us and said Mr. Morton would see us immediately. We passed through another door labeled PRIVATE and found a portly man of forty or so standing behind a polished desk in a morning coat and striped trousers. His face was as pink and shiny as a baby's. He bowed from the waist to the widow and shook my hand. It was like squeezing a rubber toy.

"Mr. Murdock, yes? I knew you were accompanying Mrs. Blackthorne. I've been reading of your exploits for a week." I'd expected his voice to squeak, but it was deep and resonant.

"Don't believe it," I said. "That twister in Nebraska already had a knot in it when I came along."

"Of course." He wasn't listening. He waved us into a pair of chairs upholstered in blue leather. Mrs. Blackthorne sat as always with back straight and her hands resting on the black reticule in her lap. The usual refreshments offered and declined, Morton tossed his tails and seated himself.

A leather portfolio, blue also, was flayed open on the desk. He glanced down at it, more with the air of confirming its presence than to consult what it contained, and folded his hands on the top sheet. From that point on I wasn't in the room.

"How much do you know of your late husband's finances?"

The widow showed no expression. "He had an army pension from his service in the war with Mexico, and a promised stipend upon his retirement. As you know, he did not live to collect it. The house in Helena is government property. We were granted its use until such time as his tenure ended; which of course it has. Apart from our savings of some two thousand, there is nothing."

"That is not the case. At the time of his, er, passing, his

interest in the Pennsylvania Railroad came to"—he spread his hands and looked down at the sheet—"twelve thousand, four hundred sixty-eight dollars and forty-two—forty-*three* cents."

"A mistake has been made, Mr. Morton. My husband refused to have any personal dealings with the railroads. The perception of influence was detrimental to a man in his position."

"So he informed us, when we advised him to invest in the Northern Pacific when it began construction in Montana Territory in 'seventy-nine. We then suggested that an eastern firm would have little to gain politically from a relationship with a federal judge so far removed from its, er, sphere. He responded with a modest purchase—ten shares, to be precise—which when the line opened the Congressional Limited with a route between New York and Philadelphia in eighteen eighty-five, rose significantly in value, and have been in the ascendance ever since. Combine that with his holdings—"

Her fingers tightened on her reticule. "He had more?"

"Nothing else so impressive, I'm afraid. A large dairy farm in Ohio, an ice plant in New York State, a limited partnership in a Baltimore shipping firm: Some four thousand and change at last report, paying three percent per annum. Not a fabulous figure in terms of a Vanderbilt, perhaps; but sufficient to keep you in substantial comfort for the rest of your days." He slapped shut the portfolio. "One thing more."

"Indeed. I thought there would be no end."

Morton rose, excusing himself, and pulled open a drawer in an oaken file cabinet. From it he took a small brown envelope with a gum flap, which he pried open with a rounded thumbnail and slid its contents onto the desk. It was a brass key.

Mrs. Blackthorne left it where it was. "I suppose that opens the door to the United States Treasury."

"Not so grand as that. It belongs to a townhouse in Wilmington, Delaware. Judge Blackthorne authorized us to purchase it in your name six months ago. It's ready for habitation at any time. At the Judge's bequest, we've arranged for your furniture and other belongings to be transported from Helena at your convenience. I can assure you there will be no obstacles from Probate; you are the only living heir, the Judge was demonstrably of sound mind, and we here at Morton, Winslow, and Morton specialize in drawing up wills. We will proceed with the reading, but it was our client's wish that you be informed of these details directly."

"The old devil," said Beatrice Blackthorne.

THIRTY-ONE

————

The old devil," she said again, when we were back in the carriage reversing our journey across the river. "All these years he let me go on thinking our existence was hand-to-mouth. 'Our service is our reward, Bea,' he said, more times than I care to remember. He made it sound as if we ran a vicarage."

I watched a flatboat carrying logs downstream. They were stacked nearly as high as the bridge, with a man standing on top to make sure they cleared. "Now that I think about it," I said, "I never heard him talk about money, except as a motive for whatever crime he was trying. It's an intimate subject for some people, like religious devotion."

"Did you ever know him to avoid a subject because of embarrassment?"

"No. He was a tough nut to crack."

"Some nuts reveal their secrets when you hold the shells up to the light. I realize now that Harlan did not trust me to stand beside him in his commitment to duty. He thought if I knew he could leave the bench at any time, I would berate him until he surrendered."

"He'd never have done that."

"I must accept some of the blame," she said. "I never made a secret of my convictions and my concerns. But I would have stayed." The words were nearly lost in the clatter of hooves. "I would have stayed."

We finished crossing the bridge in silence.

She gathered herself, squaring her hands on the bag in her lap. "We spoke of your future, back at the beginning. Have you arrived at a conclusion?"

"I've hardly had time," I said.

"If I am as wealthy as Morton claims, I shall need someone to look after my interests."

"I'm no banker. I can work a sum three times and come up with the same wrong answer each time."

"I am certain the august firm of Morton, Winslow, and Morton will know whom to hire to keep the figures. The man I need is one who can ensure whoever does keeps to the straight and narrow."

"Keep track of who comes into the office wearing a diamond stickpin on four hundred a year?"

"I did not say it would be as much of a challenge as midnight rides and fatal assignations in establishments where liquor is sold. I had the impression you were weary of that life."

"I would be, if that was all there was to it." I looked down at my boots, smiled. "Thank you, Mrs. Blackthorne, but I must decline your generous offer."

"I am not the pinchpenny the Judge was. You would be well compensated, and you need never worry about being dispatched to some forsaken place with no promise that you would return."

"You make it difficult to say no."

We'd turned down a narrow street I didn't recognize, made nearly dark as night by the buildings crowding us on both sides. I looked ahead at the man holding the lines.

"Does that mean we have an agreement?"

I slid the Deane-Adams from my belt; lowered my voice. "That isn't the man who drove us to St. Paul."

The carriage stopped with a lurch that threw us both against the back of the driver's seat. I looked at Mrs. Blackthorne to see if she was all right. That was a mistake. When I returned my attention to the man in the driver's seat, I peered down the octagonal muzzle of a long-barreled revolver. I gripped mine tightly; but the back of the seat stood in my field of fire.

The driver had read my thoughts. "I'd not chance it, friend. This packs a lot more punch than that little Marston I tickled your toes with in the livery stable."

I might have tried it, but as if to underscore his warning, he cheated the barrel to my left, where Mrs. Blackthorne sat huddled against me. I lowered my weapon and took the hammer off cock.

"Good. Pam said you were smart. I didn't have time to mark it aboard the train; responsibilities of the job and that."

I looked into his face for the first time. I'd expected Howard Rossleigh to have left his whiskers behind, but we who rode for the Judge knew about such things as ears and noses and eye color. None of them belonged to the journalist. The man wearing the cutaway coat and plug hat of a hired carriage driver was our lost conductor, known to us as Christopher

Stedman, whose body had been found floating in the Missouri
River near Bismarck.

I remembered thinking he was young for his job; but then
everyone I'd met in recent years seemed to be positively
blooming with youth. He was slim and tall—not so much as
Rossleigh, but in form and figure they were close enough to
pass for each other, provided the reporter's beard was cut off
and his features altered by bloat and ravenous fish.

We were stopped in an alley belonging to a residential
neighborhood; not one that prospered. The backs of tenement
houses were smudged with soot, layered as if by trowels from
locomotives passing within a block. The rumble and squeal of
steel wheels on steel tracks was almost constant, so that the
odd silence between trains made my ears ache. There would
be little street traffic during working hours, and jobless ten-
ants wouldn't mess with what happened outside their windows. It was as good a place to dispose of someone as the
plains of North Dakota.

I laughed, a short bark. The thin face under the stovepipe
crown went dangerously blank. He sat sideways with an arm
resting across the back of the seat and his gun hand propped
on the forearm. "Something funny, friend?"

"A little. All this time we've been looking for Howard
Rossleigh, the murderer of our conductor, and all this time he's
been feeding eels."

"A change of clothes and a razor bought us a breather. I
spun that stowaway yarn to soften you up for what came.
Rossleigh would still be scribbling if he hadn't recognized me
in the caboose; I seen it the first time, and the second when

he placed me. I was a brakeman with the U.P. till I passed out drunk on the job and we jumped the tracks going too fast round a bend. Some people died; he covered my trial. The jury hung, so I didn't. Quiet work, Rossleigh; I'm near as good with a blade as with a gun. Nobody'll find the real Stedman. *That* wasn't a body I wanted found."

"Dear Lord." Mrs. Blackthorne looked down, as if praying.

"What did Pamela Bower have to do with you?" I asked.

A smile split the thin face. It looked genuinely sad. "I see she talked before she croaked. Only the name ain't Bower, either. She took mine when we hitched up."

Mrs. Blackthorne raised her head. "You were married?"

"I don't look good enough for her, I know; but she promised to write a series of pieces clearing my name. I couldn't get a job with any railroad otherwise, and it's the only work I know. In the meantime she was pretty to have around, and Hearst pays better than the rest, so I didn't starve. I owed her plenty; still do."

I said, "If you agreed to help her kill me, why didn't you use your pistol in the stable instead of her Marston?"

"I wasn't to kill you; though I could have, even with that toy. You get a lot of practice shooting rats from on top of freight cars; people are pigs when it comes to throwing their garbage alongside the tracks. She gave me her gun. She wanted the slug found. She knew you'd guess it came from that derringer. Why do you think she showed it to you aboard *The Javelin*? She wanted to make sure you knew who was out for your neck, keep you guessing why till she got the chance to tell you."

I asked how they'd managed to conjure up a balloon.

He blew air from back in his throat. He probably thought it was a laugh.

"A stroke, that's what that was. We could've caught up with you easy, but then that feller touched down by the lumber camp offering rides at a dollar a head, and Pam said we could pass you and catch you with your pants down. We got our money's worth, once we was up in the air with no place for the feller to run out of range. He was happy enough to get shut of us once we passed you."

"Pam's dead," I said. "Why keep it up now?"

The smile sloughed from his face. I thought his eyes glistened. "It's the only thing she asked me to do when we got married. 'All this,' she said, 'your rescue, my support, our companionship, in return for this one small thing.'"

Beatrice said, "You loved her."

His features twisted, as if she'd slapped him. He lunged, snatched hold of her high collar, jerked her close, and buried the barrel of the big revolver in the flesh under her chin. "Drop it, Murdock!"

When I hesitated, his voice rose to a shriek. "By God, hers'll be the shortest widowhood in the book!"

I opened my hand, letting the Deane-Adams fall to the floor of the carriage with a thump.

"Funny. I was going to say the same thing about you."

This was a new voice. A man stood silhouetted against the sunlight at the far end of the alley, feet wide apart. His face and figure were a blank, but he wore a medium-brim hat with a low crown, a hip-length coat with the tails spread, and the light painted a bright line along the barrel of a carbine with the butt nestled in the hollow of his right shoulder.

The brakeman's back was turned his way. His eyes were wild now. He tightened his grip on the woman's collar, dug the muzzle deeper into her neck. She made strangling noises.

"*Drop it!*" bellowed the stranger.

Look to his eye. A dead man's voice, advising me from a grave grown over for twenty years.

I said before it's the hands you watch, not the eyes; but I knew where his hands were, and I'd forgotten that first time back in Helena. I spotted the moment when the hot irises shifted, toward the source of the shout. I backhanded Mrs. Blackthorne hard across the cheek. She cried out, jerking and knocking the gun away from her neck. As that was happening I snatched up the Deane-Adams and shot the brakeman through the left eye.

THIRTY-TWO

The beergardens of Minneapolis, if this one was any indication, were cozy dark caves, paneled and furnished in black walnut, with lamps shaded to an ember glow and a fug of tobacco smoke and bitter ale built stratum upon stratum over decades. Deputy U.S. Marshal Hosea Johnston and I sat in a leather-upholstered horseshoe near a fireplace where logs belched and crackled as they burned; it was spring, but there was a stiff wind scraping off Lake Superior, bringing in its chill every time someone opened the street door and brightening the flames in the glass chimneys. We had tankards in front of us, like pirates in storybooks, and a thin cigar smoldered between my companion's fingers. How he kept it burning was a mystery; I never once saw him bring it up to his lips after he got it lit.

He was in his middle thirties, although his face looked older, cured by sun and wind and smoked over campfires. A solid black bar of eyebrow gave a false impression of humorlessness; his sense of irony was sound. With it came a Quakerish beard, no moustaches, and the low-crowned hat I'd seen in the alley, inexplicably the headpiece of a town-dweller, pearl-gray felt with a modest brim and a silk band. His coat, at least, was rural, a mackinaw with faded squares and mismatched buttons. The nickel-plated star of the Brotherhood drooped from the flap pocket of his frayed shirt.

"I gambled it was you he wanted," he said, turning the tankard between his palms without disturbing the ash on the end of his cigar. "You or Mrs. Blackthorne. When I found out Stedman's wallet with his railroad card was wrapped in oilskin, I knew whoever put it there meant it to be read after they dragged the body from the water. That's when he stopped being Stedman and started being Rossleigh."

"Another gamble," I said.

"Not so much. Two men dropping out of sight at the same time could be a coincidence. Three would be like drawing to an inside straight. No. You have to be certain about something, even if it turns out you were wrong. Am I right?" He lifted his tankard, skimming off the foam with his thumb as he did so, drank. "He could just as easily have dropped that hammer on the widow when you struck her in the face."

"It worked once before," I said, "a long time ago. I never said there was anything wrong with gambling. I didn't know who you were, or what kind of shot, or if I'd have to deal with you after the brakeman. No one knows all the odds when he plays them."

"I doubt the lady will see things that way. She's going to have a honey of a shiner."

"You don't know this lady."

He looked at the magic cigar, still lisping smoke. He tilted it into a brass ashtray, breaking off two inches of ash. "My mother named me from a book of the Bible. Maybe you know it."

"I read it whenever I'm in need of a nightmare."

"The Lord sure could hold a grudge."

I grinned. "Who hasn't had a boss like that?"

He went on twisting out the cigar. "Reason I asked, I'm a God-fearing man myself and can use more in my camp. World out here's changed. There's no room in the service for men without some kind of standard. Those who have it are too slow to strike, and those who don't, strike without regard to the penalty."

"You don't want me. You want Frank Merriwell."

"Hear me out. The man Jack Rimfire and those others used to write about, that's not a man I'd have. The man I'd have is the one I've been hearing about these last several years." He looked up at me from under his black bar of brow. "We need you in the Dakotas. I could talk to the marshal."

"Thanks. I've got a job."

"The one you said the lady offered? Kind of tame for you, isn't it?"

"I meant the one in Helena."

"Be working for some thinned-out bureaucrat, no Blackthorne."

"Blackthorne wasn't Blackthorne when I met him. Not quite. I put on the finishing touches."

"Back then you had that kind of time."

A flatulent horn sounded outside, accompanied by the cough and sputter of a combustion engine.

"Back then we all did." I drank my beer.

———

Funerals bring out the worst in me; the worst kind of man, that is. I always expect the minister to be smooth-faced and glib, his selection from Scripture as bland as boiled fish, the sobbing of the mourners timed to the moment, as in a play that had run too long.

The graveside ceremony in the Presbyterian churchyard in Wilmington was therefore a disappointment. The clergyman was young and devout, and although he could not have known the deceased personally—having been born several years after the Blackthornes had decamped to Montana—he had done his spadework, and found positive parallels between his devotion to duty and the sixth book of the Old Testament:

> *And when the Lord raised them up judges, then the Lord was with the judge, and delivered them out of the hand of their enemies all the days of the judge; for it repented the Lord because of their groanings by reason of them that oppressed them and vexed them.*

There was little weeping, but all heads bowed and no impatient congress with pocket watches. I recognized among the pallbearers two senators (one a sworn Blackthorne enemy) and a member of the House of Representatives by their likenesses in newspapers, and guessed a similar affiliation in the others by their dress and shaped whiskers, and Mrs. Blackthorne told me that she'd found a wire waiting for her sent by President Cleveland expressing sympathy and apologies that affairs of state would not allow him to attend the service. Officers with the District of Columbia Police Department, mounted and on foot, kept crowds of the curious from passing through the surrounding iron fence.

The sky was bright, something that always depressed me

when someone was laid to rest beneath it. The Judge would have found wry satisfaction in a scene of cerecloth clouds, icy rain, and black umbrellas. He'd have said, "At least it's one pleasant day I didn't miss."

When the box was lowered by straps into the ground and the last of us had deposited his fistful of earth on the lid, Beatrice Blackthorne took my arm in her gloved hand and we walked away, pausing from time to time while she accepted condolences with an obligatory nod and wan smile.

"It would have amused him to know Claypool was forced to support him in the end," she said.

Claypool was the name of the senator who'd spent most of his time on the floor of Congress denouncing the Judge.

"Don't try to fool a fooler, ma'am. It wouldn't have happened if he hadn't arranged it at the same time he roped me into this trip."

"Nor would *that* have happened if he hadn't anticipated danger of some kind. You were the man he considered most worthy of his trust."

"I was the one who supplied the danger, don't forget."

"I have not forgotten. I remember also that you were the one who brought it to an end. I am sorry you turned down my offer. It would have pleased Harlan to know I was still in your care."

"Don't try to blackmail me, ma'am. He'd have busted a gut to know I fell for it."

She raised a hand to her veil, touching the bruise on her cheek. "No man ever struck me before. He would have taken a horsewhip to any who did."

I fancied I could hear waves walloping the shore of the bay, my first experience of the Atlantic Ocean. It was probably the Delaware River flowing round a snag.

"Is it always like this here?" I said. "I'd thought it a rainy place."

"You are a most infuriating man. To attempt to move you to anger is to invite a comment on the weather. Of course I know you saved my life. Might you have found a better way?"

"I'm sure of it. I'm sloppy when pressed."

Before helping her into our waiting carriage I took a long look at the driver. He was the same one who had brought us.

I said, "Where to, the townhouse?" She'd checked out of the hotel.

"I would have to sleep on the floor. All our—*my* furniture is still in Helena, and I have had my life's portion of hotel life and berths aboard trains. I will direct you to my sister's house."

We clip-clopped along the well-ordered streets. The air was a mix of piped gas and coal smoke. An army of streetsweeps bore away horse-apples before they could contribute much to the atmosphere.

She seemed to have followed my thoughts. "Is it so horrible here? Too settled a place for so shaggy a wolf as you?"

No place for one that would kill its own flesh.

Aloud I said, "You've been reading the Hearst press. I'm as homebody as they come. It isn't my fault home's not here."

She patted my arm.

"You are more like Harlan than you care to admit."

First class, I thought; though I didn't say it.